Pride Publishing books by Angel Martinez

Wild Rose, Silent Snow
Boots

Offbeat Crimes
Lime Gelatin and Other Monsters
The Pill Bugs of Time
Skim Blood and Savage Verse
Feral Dust Bunnies
Jackalopes and Woofen-Poofs

AURA
Quinn's Gambit
Flax's Pursuit
Kellen's Awakening

Anthologies
50s Mixed Tape: The Line

Offbeat Crimes

JACKALOPES AND WOOFEN-POOFS

ANGEL MARTINEZ

Jackalopes and Woofen-Poofs
ISBN # 978-1-78686-325-6
©Copyright Angel Martinez 2017
Cover Art by Posh Gosh ©Copyright October 2017
Interior text design by Claire Siemaszkiewicz
Pride Publishing

Published in 2017 by Pride Publishing, Think Tank, Ruston Way, Lincoln, LN6 7FL, United Kingdom.

Pride Publishing is an imprint of Totally Entwined Group Limited.

JACKALOPES
AND
WOOFEN-POOFS

Dedication

To families everywhere who love their children as they are and to those who make the effort to learn when their children surprise them.

Chapter One

The alarm went off a full hour and a half earlier than normal. Wolf snarled and buried his face against Jason's naked shoulder.

"That was a legit Big Bad Wolf sound," Jason murmured as he rolled over and wrapped his arms around Wolf. Two seconds later, his eyes shot open. "Crap. You have to get to State today. Up. Get up."

"But it's nicer here." Wolf turned his head away for a yawn-whine, conscious of unbrushed teeth.

"I'm not gonna give your mom a reason to say I'm a bad influence." Jason, on the wall side of the bed, shoved hard enough to push Wolf to the edge.

"Fine. I'm up. I really don't want to do this."

The *pip-tick* of the central air starting up whispered from the vents. *Great. Just great.* Beginning of October and it was still hot and humid enough to kick the air on at four in the morning. Jason's hand stroking his back was both a comfort and a temptation, but just as he'd resolved to lie back down for one more snuggle, the muted thunder of tiny paws came galloping up the stairs.

Audacity careened around the corner, meowing like a miniature air raid siren, her black tabby coloring nearly invisible in the darkened bedroom. She'd heard the alarm, of course, and was coming to scold him for still being in bed.

Wolf scooped her up to prevent her from setting her claws against his bare legs and carried her to the bathroom, where he placed her on the vanity. His kitten insisted on supervising his showers and would cry bloody murder if he locked her out. She seemed convinced he might drown if she wasn't there to watch him.

The whole squad had been dreading this day. Going up to State Paranormal to answer the board's questions about a case was never fun — not that it happened a lot. Unless Wolf's squad had interesting specimens to send, State usually acted like the 77th wasn't worth the attention a mosquito would rate. Every so often, they'd call someone up to answer questions about a weird case, like when Carrington had made the trip to Harrisburg to answer questions about the word-spitting books.

But this? This would be a board of inquiry and one of the 77th's best officers was in the line of fire. Wolf found he resented that.

Just as he had finished rinsing off and was letting the hot water pound against his knotted shoulders, a black paw batted its way around the end of the shower curtain.

Miieew.

"All right, little girl, I'm coming." Wolf shut off the faucets, wiping water from his eyes. "I don't get an extra couple of minutes today?"

The answer was short and prim. *Mew.*

"That sounds like a no." He reached over her for the towel while she swiped at the drops falling from his arm. When she stood on her hind legs to try to lick at the shower curtain, he pointed at her. "No shower curtain water. You have nice water in your dish."

Miiiw.

"I don't care. It's gross. And probably soapy."

She sneezed and sat down on the bathmat to wait for him, not at all distressed as some cats might have been at the drips falling on her. When he got out his electric razor, she jumped onto the toilet lid and from there back to the vanity, where she purred as if encouraging the shaver while he ran it over his face.

"You can't come to work with me today, you know."

Miw.

He didn't think she understood everything he said but he still talked to her as if she did. Just in case. She certainly seemed to understand a lot.

Downstairs, Mom was already in the kitchen with a pot of coffee and eggs and bacon on the stove. Jason, in a T-shirt and pajama bottoms, puttered around setting the table and handling all the non-cooking parts of breakfast like toast and juice.

The domestic scene was so peaceful and cozy, so like *family* that the backs of Wolf's eyes stung. It had been just him and his mom for so long... Well, it was wonderful. That's what it was. Even though he felt guilty since Dad wasn't there.

"Mom, you didn't have to get up this early."

She half-turned to give him a look. "And have you two eating cereal for breakfast? No, you need something fortifying today. I wasn't sleeping anyway."

Jason gave him a swift kiss and handed him a glass of orange juice. "Miriam's afraid I'll make a disaster area out of her kitchen if I try to cook for you."

"I never said that," Mom said with mock-severity.

"You were thinking it and you wouldn't be wrong," Jason chuckled. "Alex, you're not in trouble, are you? With this hearing?"

Wolf shook his head as he took his seat at the table. Audacity climbed into the chair beside him, watching proceedings with her ears swiveling. Mom had already fed her or she would have been batting at the fridge for her breakfast. "Not directly. No. I have to testify, though. I hate this."

"I think Kash did the right thing," Mom said as she scooped eggs and bacon onto three plates and broke up one small piece of bacon into tiny pieces on a fourth. "And if those snooty people at State think they could've done better, they should come and help out here once in a while. Not that they care what I think, of course."

Audacity started on her bacon as soon as Mom set the plate in front of her. She was meticulously polite, only putting one paw on the table and taking a piece at a time. Jason had frowned at encouraging a cat to eat at the table but Mom had said her granddaughter could have something with the grownups if she behaved. So Audacity did.

"Kinda wish I could take you with me, Mom," Wolf mumbled around a bite of toast.

"I wish I could go too, sweetie. But then all the other officers would want to take their moms and the poor board of inquiry members at State probably wouldn't survive."

"Makes me shudder thinking about it," Jason said with a laugh. He turned the conversation to a new restaurant and Wolf was grateful for the distraction, reaching across to cover Jason's hand with his.

Warm. Loved. Staying right here all day would suit him just fine.

He couldn't, of course. Breakfast over, he trudged back upstairs to get into his summer uniform, all crisp and sharp from being ironed the night before. It wouldn't be a fun trip, but he was determined not to be an embarrassment to his department.

Jason let out a low wolf whistle when he came back down, so he knew he looked good. Or maybe Jason was trying to make him feel better. Mom held Audacity in her arms, explaining once again that she could *not* go to work with Daddy that day, while Jason handed him his hat and keys and gave him a soft kiss for the road. Even that brief kiss melted the ice lodged in his stomach so he could manage a smile for them.

Everything felt backward and upside-down. On days when Jason had stayed over, it was usually Wolf and his mom seeing him out the door so he could get home, let the dogs out, feed all his animal friends and still make it to work on time.

The warm light from the doorway and his little cobbled-together family waving from the top step only served to heighten his sense of dislocation and isolation. All his instincts screamed at him that this wasn't going to be a good day.

* * * *

"No. No strategies." Kash stood ramrod straight, his face etched in stone. "Be honest and don't think about what someone else might have said or didn't say. They will expect some discrepancies from eyewitnesses."

Kyle, in contrast to his serene-seeming partner, looked close to a stroke. "But we need —"

"If anyone goes down in flames here, it's me. No collateral damage."

They stood in the lobby of SPHQ, under the black marble columns chased in gold and the rotunda thirty feet above them, decorated with battling figures Wolf couldn't make out. The décor was meant to intimidate and impress but it struck him as out of place for a police headquarters. Too... There was a word he couldn't think of. Started with an *O*. Carrington would've known.

Only Carrington and Vance were missing from their group, since Carrington had been at the hospital that evening, frantic about Erasmus, and Vance had been in no shape for any more action after burning the giant dust bunny to cinders. Two members of their squad safe, at least.

"Kash, I get that you want to be noble and take the fall for us," Jeff said softly. "But I was senior at the site that day."

Kash stepped over to Jeff, the movement sudden and shocking as he loomed, crowding Jeff. "Why didn't you stop me? They'll ask that, Jeff."

"I... You *know* why," Jeff whispered.

"Hmm." Kash stepped back, the unassuming statue again.

This wasn't the Vikash Soren they knew — reserved, yes, but he was always polite and friendly. Despite his calm exterior, Kash's sharp, chilly treatment of his squad mates had to be a signal of how nervous he was. Wolf chewed on his lower lip, his jaws aching to gnaw on something with more abandon like a rawhide or a table leg to ease his own nerves. Yes, he knew what Kash meant. He'd been the only one of them to have a full year as a detective before he had been flagged as an unclassifiable paranormal, his rank knocked back and his assignment transferred to Philly because State Paranormal didn't know what to do with him. Except for Carrington, they had all gravitated toward thinking Kash outranked them. It just felt right.

Wolf sighed, trying not to breathe too deeply. He hated the smell of the place. Not that the pristine building stank, not in any way a normal human would pick up, but it disturbed him. The dry cedar smell of the oldest vamps was bad enough — the presence of powerful predators always raised the hairs on his arms. The stench of werewolf musk was even worse. They were just so *mean*. Mom said they had testosterone poisoning, even the females.

A cadet in SP black skidded around one of the columns, trying to keep a ball in the air above his palm. With a dark frown, Shira sidestepped the kid. She was probably having all sorts of feelings about someone who could control their telekinesis. Sort of. A vamp captain concentrating on a sheaf of paperwork as he headed for the stairs wasn't as lucky. A sudden lurch after the ball slammed the cadet into him and sent them both sprawling while the red rubber ball bounced gleefully away.

Wolf had to lock his knees not to chase it. Krisk's hand on his shoulder helped.

"So much for vamp grace," Amanda muttered, though she knew better than anyone how good vampire hearing was.

There was a bit of flailing amid the tangle of black uniformed limbs before the captain freed himself and leapt to his feet, hissing and showing fangs. He spared a sharp glare for Amanda but saved his full threat display for the cadet, now scrabbling backward along the black marble, clearly desperate for distance. Acting on instinct and not much sense, Wolf stepped between them, his first impulse being to protect the cub.

The vampire captain met his interference with a deep-chested, apex predator growl. Wolf tried to stop himself, horrified when a louder growl crawled up his own throat. *I should back off. I can't back off. He'll lunge. I need to back off. He outranks me.*

"Oh, my goodness. Sir, are you all right?" Shira popped up between them, doing her best blonde and blue-eyed innocent impression and holding out the captain's scattered notes. "That was quite a fall. The cadet's fine. I hope I haven't disarranged your notes too badly."

Across the lobby, an ornamental iron lamp clattered to the floor. The outer doors crashed open. Shira might have seemed calm but her stress telekinesis had gone into overdrive.

"Thank you, my dear. I'm unharmed." The captain took the papers from her, his demeanor shifting from feral to puzzled gentility. "I do suggest you keep a tighter leash on your dog, though."

The insult irritated Wolf but even he knew it was childish. Tense relations between vamps and werewolves had always been a problem at State, but Wolf wasn't some surly were. He backed off now that the threat level had de-escalated.

"Cadet Nelson!" the captain leaned around Shira to yell. "You addle-pated hoser! What in the gods' names did you think you were doing?"

Shira shot Wolf a 'he did not just say that' look that he completely understood. The older vamps had some weird language issues but hearing Shakespearean insults snuggled up against 80s slang was jarring.

"Sir!" Nelson scrambled to his feet to offer a shaky salute. "Instructor Carpenter said I need to practice whenever I can. She said if I can't get control, I'll get sent down to the freaks in the 77th."

"Nice," Kyle said under his breath.

The vampire captain—Valbuena, his nameplate read—made a strangled sound and turned it into a cough. "Ah, cadets. Sometimes I'd like to drown the lot of them." He raised his voice to address the hapless youngster still standing at attention. "You will *not* practice in any common, populated area, Nelson. You are a menace. And learn your damn insignia. These officers are 77th."

All the color drained from Nelson's face. Poor kid looked like he was going to be sick as he stammered through a disjointed apology.

"Go on. Retrieve your toy and get out of my sight, Cadet."

Almost as one being, they watched the cadet scramble for his ball and hurry off. When he was out of sight, Captain Valbuena turned back to Shira. "Can I help you find something, Officer Lourdes?"

"No, sir. Thank you. We're on our way up to the board room for a hearing."

His eyes narrowed and the cedar scent rolling off him sharpened. "Disciplinary?"

"Board of inquiry," Kash answered.

"Ah. I won't keep you then." He offered Shira an ironic little bow and a dazzling smile. "Ma'am. Lovely to meet you."

Someone was growling as Captain Valbuena walked away and it wasn't Wolf. He looked around at his colleagues and found Greg to be the growl source.

"Self-important, jumped-up leech," Greg spat out.

Wolf hadn't thought the vamp had been *that* bad. Oh, wait. Shira was fire-engine red, her jaw locked tight. Captain Valbuena hadn't just been polite to her, Wolf guessed. He so often missed human flirting. Vampire flirting was apparently even harder for him to pick up.

"There, there, Greg." Kyle slung an arm around Greg and started them all walking toward the grand staircase again. "Just because he was better looking and had better diction."

"Oh, shut up, Monroe."

"He was plastering it on with a putty knife," Shira offered. "I'll take *our* vampire over these SP creeps any day."

"And ours is super gay, so no competition," Amanda said with a laugh. "Oh, that poor kid. I remember how not fun being a cadet here was."

"Were you?" Kash asked in a distracted fashion.

"Yeah. Did it backwards, though. Most times, you cadet first, then go through the police academy. I'd gone through the academy before they figured out I could do extra shit."

"Wait. So you had to go back to being a cadet?" Kyle gaped at her. "That's not right."

Amanda shrugged, her gaze focused on a point at the top of the stairs. "The pre-cogs get fast-tracked. Everyone else — people who can tell stuff from touching shit, I can't ever remember the word for it, other people who can see stuff in the past like me — we all get tested. If it's not good enough, they put you in training."

"They did it with me, too," Shira murmured. "Lack of control."

"I didn't know that." Greg bumped shoulders with her.

"Anyway. Didn't mean to bring everybody down." Amanda frowned at the stairs and started taking two at a time. "My paranormal stuff was too wonky, too unpredictable, and they figured out I only see a day or two back into stuff that's happened if I get anything. So they let me get back to being a cop."

Shira craned her head around, searching from face to face. "Nobody else?"

"Not me." Jeff shook his head. "They knew the day they hauled me in for testing that I was a freak. I've been throwing fruit around with my brain since I was a kid and knew I couldn't move anything else. Got labeled DPT — *defective paranormal talent* — and reassigned the same day. Same story for Vance. To come to us, you're either defective, unclassifiable or what they so kindly call *physiologically alternative*, like Wolf and Krisk."

Greg raised a hand. "Defective."

"Unclassifiable," Kash chimed in, pointing between himself and Kyle.

"So is our vamp defective or alternative?" Kyle asked.

Amanda rolled her eyes. "Don't you ever ask that where he can hear you unless you want a long rant filled with big words. State has Carr down as defective. He fought them on it, saying he was just a new kind of vamp. He lost."

"Ouch." Kyle cringed. "But wasn't he stuck here at State for a while? Did they bump him to cadet?"

Jeff shook his head as he reached the top step. "Carr's issues aren't ones you can train away and that was before they formed the 77th. He was the first officer assigned. I was the second. Before our department came along, they would've just fired us when we were outed as paranormal."

"At least we have *our* 77th here." Shira huffed. "Other states' 77ths take the local paranormals for that city, the regular ones. They don't keep defectives on the force at all."

Kash stopped so abruptly on the landing that Wolf nearly ran into him. "Yes. Why *is* that?"

No one had an answer for him, so he shook his head and strode on, the small crease between his eyebrows the only sign that he struggled with something. Wolf figured he was worried. He got that. Visits to State always made him uncomfortable, and a visit where they had to explain an incident worried him, too. All this talk about firing. He knew the board wouldn't fire them all. Probably not. But losing Kash would be awful.

They signed in with a desk sergeant in the antechamber and were told to wait. Wolf had only been up to the boardroom twice, once right after graduating from the Academy and once to stand witness to what had happened the night a monster alligator snapping turtle had exploded. He was convinced that the vampires at State had done all the building's interiors. Everything was so dark and...dark.

The antechamber matched the boardroom with its deep-umber wood paneling and its—he hated to say it—blood red carpets. Wrought iron sconces lined the walls, but the only real light was the pool around the sergeant's desk with its computer and friendlier desk lamp. Normal vampire tastes didn't seem terribly subtle, or maybe the décor was just meant to intimidate. It did manage that.

Wolf muffled a sneeze against his arm. *Damn it.* No way to get around being in the same room with the board vamps and weres, but he'd hoped he wouldn't start sneezing so soon. Krisk handed him a tissue with what might have been a sympathetic nod.

The sergeant finally let them in twenty minutes after their appointed time and they all filed into an even gloomier room than the antechamber. No sconces or windows interrupted the boardroom walls. Four pools of light provided the only illumination—the lamp fixed to the left side of the single desk facing the board members' long table and the three desk lamps at each of the human board member's seats in the middle of that table. The two vampire board members sat on the far right, the two werewolf members on the left, as far away from each other as they could while still sitting at the same table.

"Please take seats, Officers." The older human woman at the center of the table, Commander Rahway, if Wolf remembered right, pointed to the rows of chairs at the back of the room. "We'll call you as we need you."

With several murmured *yes, ma'ams*, they filed into seats, waiting while the board members conferred in lowered voices and shuffled papers.

The commander peered over her half-moon glasses at the paper in her hand. "Hmm. Yes. Let's have Officer Gatling first, please."

Jeff's cheeks expanded on a blown-out breath as he rose reluctantly. He stalked to the desk in the middle of the room like a man going to the gallows where he offered the board a sharp salute before the commander told him to sit.

Commander Rahway had returned to paper shuffling. "Let the record show that this board of inquiry has been convened to examine events that occurred within the closed riverfront powerplant known as the Delaware Station. Please state your name and department."

"Officer Jeffrey Gatling, ma'am. 77th precinct, Philadelphia."

"No need to *ma'am* me into next week, Officer. You will be addressing the board." She waved a hand to indicate the people at the table as she rattled through names. "In addition, let the record show the following presiding over this board of inquiry—Colonel Valbuena, Major Firenz, Colonel Hawthorne, Major Pak, Colonel Bjorstad, Major O'Donnell, and myself. Officer Gatling, I understand you were the senior onsite that evening?"

"Yes, m—that is, I was."

Wolf lost most of Jeff's run through of what had happened that day, both at the engagement party where the huge dust bunny had attacked, and later at the abandoned power plant where Kash had destroyed the arcane laboratory in which the rabid dust bunnies were being created. He was still stuck on Colonel Valbuena and the captain they'd met downstairs. It wasn't a human name one heard a lot, like Jones or Rodriguez. Were they brothers? Cousins, maybe, since they didn't look anything alike? And both of them vampires? Did that happen with some families?

By the time he resurfaced from his wondering about hawk-nosed, Mediterranean vampires versus golden, more WASP-y looking ones, Jeff's testimony was nearly complete. Wolf was glad for the dim room and hoped his heated face didn't glow in the dark.

They only had two more questions for Jeff and if his fists suddenly clenching on the table were any indication, it hit like a bat to the back of the head.

"Officer Gatling, are you aware that destroying a site of arcane working is against regulations?" Colonel Valbuena purred with barely hidden contempt.

"Yes, sir."

"Then as the senior officer present, why didn't you stop it?"

Jeff's chin came up a hair. The scent of his nervousness rolled back to Wolf in waves but his voice was steady when he answered. "Sir, regs are clear that it's up to the officers onsite to decide whether an arcane working is a clear and present danger to civilians."

"Well." Colonel Valbuena tapped his papers straight in an obvious dismissal. "I suppose we should all be grateful that you don't have to make those decisions often then."

With Amanda, they concentrated on her post-cognitive work that had helped find the dust bunny site. Had she and Kyle tried a power boost before? How did it work? What had she seen? Again and again, asking for more precise wording, more complete descriptions. Amanda struggled, never the best with words. When they finally dismissed her, she slumped back into the chair next to Wolf, muttering about how next time she'd bring Carrington and his snooty vocabulary along.

Both Shira's and Greg's testimonies were more straightforward accountings of events. If the board members thought either of them would offer something new or would make accusations against their squad mates, they were disappointed. Krisk's testimony nearly gave some of the less patient board members fits. They weren't used to the way he said things and Wolf didn't feel it was his place to translate. No one asked, at any rate, so he felt no obligation to. Krisk typed into the tablet on the desk and the words were projected on the dark side wall of the room. He had most of them thoroughly confused by the time he typed —

Partial use of organic matter. Cannibalization of life force for continued structural integrity. Issues of possible initial life force use were disturbing.

"What the hell?" Major Pak grumbled.

Commander Rahway wasn't quite as easy to lose. She frowned at Krisk as she asked, "Is this your idea of speculation, Officer Krisk? Suggesting that live sacrifices were necessary to create the creatures?"

Krisk's tail thumped the floor in a heavy, slow rhythm. Oh, he was pissed.

Not speculation. Analysis.

"Hmm. Unless you have data to support, we can't accept it as such. Do you have anything further to add?"

All incidents are one. Only increase can be anticipated.

"Thank you, Krisk. You may step down," the commander cut across mutterings about weird lizard philosophy. "Officer Wolf, if you please."

Wolf got an encouraging pat from Krisk as they switched places. The spot in the center of the room felt so isolated in its little puddle of light and Wolf struggled to sit straight and still, trying not to let his nerves show.

The werewolf officers didn't make things any easier as the colonel leaned close to the major and whispered, "I smell wet dog."

Major O'Donnell whispered back, "Aren't there leash regs in this building?"

Cool and cultured, Colonel Valbuena spoke from the other end of the table, "You *do* know the officer's hearing is most likely better than yours?"

"Keep your nose where it belongs, you giant tick," O'Donnell muttered to the table.

The humans couldn't have heard the exchange, but Commander Rahway looked around in alarm as the other vampire, Major Firenz, rose from his chair to snarl, "Apologize to the colonel, you cur."

"Gentlemen, please. Not now," the commander hissed.

O'Donnell was up now, his green eyes giving off an unhealthy red glow. Wolf pulled in deep, even breaths as he tried to keep himself from echoing the growls issuing from the front of the room. It was damn hard. The air crackled with threat and his human friends behind him would be vulnerable if this got ugly. O'Donnell and Firenz were going to go for each other. *Any second now.*

As O'Donnell leaped, Commander Rahway moved much faster than her elderly body suggested she could. She sprang to her feet, hands snapping out to either side. Papers to her right rustled, seemingly on their own. They rolled up and rose to just above shoulder height. At the same moment on her left, a portable work light with its cord appeared from beneath the table like a metal cobra rising from a basket.

The rolled up papers smacked O'Donnell hard on the nose and he reared back, shocked and indignant. The work light switched on directly in Firenz's face. He stumbled back with a sharp cry, one hand thrown up to block the light.

"Gentlemen, resume your seats," the commander ordered in an icy tone.

Wolf snapped his mouth shut when he realized it hung open. He knew there were powerful psychics at State but he'd never seen such precise, lightning-fast telekinesis in action. Probably not something he should say to Shira later. Or ever. Major O'Donnell was still rubbing his nose as he subsided. Major Firenz had his head in both hands as he resumed his seat. Not someone a person wanted to tick off, Commander Rahway.

"Now then." The commander smoothed her iron gray hair back. "Officer Wolf. Your colleagues have provided ample detail into most of the evening's events. But I'm a bit puzzled by references to your *leading* them to the site."

"I—" Wolf cleared his throat three times trying to rid himself of the leftover growl in his voice. "I could smell them, ma'am."

"Smell whom?"

Wolf gripped his hat tight in both hands to keep them from shaking. He'd been nervous enough before and now the adrenaline shakes from the almost-fight had him in their teeth. "The dust bunnies, ma'am."

The look she gave him was one part surprised and two parts tired-of-nonsense-today. "Officer Wolf, are you implying that you can distinguish between different *kinds* of dust scents?"

"Sometimes, ma'am. Yes. But this wasn't a regular dust scent. It was sharp. Not something you'd want to smell. Officer Loveless called it a blue cheese and unwashed socks hit by lightning smell. That's pretty damn—sorry, ma'am—close."

"I see. That certainly sounds distinctive." The commander gave him a long, thorough look. "Gentlemen? Anything additional?"

"Yes, Commander, if you'd indulge me," Colonel Valbuena responded, his soft voice barely carrying across the room. "Officer Wolf, from how far away can you detect a scent?"

"Depends on what it is, sir. I can separate out everyone's scent in this room and if someone walked away, I'd probably be able to pinpoint three rooms away."

"Impressive, though still a short distance." The colonel turned a page over, still staring at his papers rather than look at Wolf. "How is it that you were able to detect the dust creatures from more than half a mile away?"

One of the werewolves laughed and Wolf squirmed, fighting the urge to turn and glare. "There was a trail, sir. I can't say how old. But that's how I knew what direction to take us. I guess the dust bun—creatures were being let out to feed at some point."

"Oh, you guess, do you?" The colonel finally glanced up without raising his head. "Is this how you approach all of your police work, Officer Wolf? By guessing?"

"No, sir. Just wondered why the trail was there."

"Hmm." Colonel Valbuena returned to studying his papers, apparently having lost interest in Wolf entirely.

There were a couple more questions about what they had found inside the power plant, then the board dismissed him.

Amanda patted his leg when he sat down. "You did good. Hard part's over for you."

He appreciated the support but the worry didn't evaporate and the adrenaline shakes didn't subside. Not yet. Probably not until they were out of this building.

They were harder on Kyle, pelting questions at him rapid fire about how long he had known about the power boost ability, why he had kept it secret and how consistently it worked. Kyle tried but their tactics were enough to rattle anyone. He was close to shouting when he finally said the combining of his and Kash's talents had been in the account from the giant snapping turtle incident and if State couldn't be bothered to read the reports, that wasn't his fault. They got what they wanted with the confirmation that Kyle hadn't tried it with anyone else prior to the evening in question, and the board allowed a frazzled, red-faced Kyle to return to his seat.

"Officer Vikash Soren," Commander Rahway said without courtesies.

This was the part they'd all been dreading, but Kash took his place—cool, composed, a man carved of glacial rock. With meticulous care, the board took Kash through the whole event—where he had been, what he had done, what thoughts he'd had and what he had suggested at every point. They didn't try to rattle him like they had Kyle. Maybe they knew it wouldn't work. They did seem to be trying to wear him down, trip him up.

Kash stood firm on every point, never stumbling, never backtracking. It was a little scary. Finally, they got to the point.

"Officer Soren." Commander Rahway folded her hands atop her papers. "Were you aware that what you were looking at was an arcane site?"

"Yes, ma'am."

"Were you, perhaps lacking the years of experience some of your colleagues have in a paranormal department, confused about procedure regarding such a site?"

"No, ma'am." If anything, Kash had pulled himself up straighter and looked even stonier. "The regulations are clear to report to State."

The other board members had gone still and quiet, apparently waiting for the commander to go in for the kill. "Then would you please explain why you believed it appropriate, against regulations, against advice, to destroy the site?"

"Yes, ma'am. The creatures created at this site were a clear and imminent danger—to civilians, to my—our officers, to the local ecosystem. While it may have been necessary for the summoner to conduct each new creation onsite, I think it's far more likely, given the setup, that the creation happened on a regular cycle. If that cycle happened nightly, we couldn't take the risk of another creation. Also, I must protest the use of the word *destroy* to describe the condition in which we left the site. The circle was disrupted, yes, but most of the pieces should still have been retrievable."

"The condition in which we left the site? Who do you include in this *we*, Soren?"

"In which *I* left the site, ma'am. My apologies. I misspoke."

Commander Rahway heaved an aggravated sigh. "Go sit down, Soren. The board members will retire and discuss. We'll return with our findings."

Kash returned to them and sank into his chair beside Kyle. For all his calm, he still looked like a man waiting for the firing squad. He waited with a huge helping of courage, but the way he shushed Kyle's questions said everything about how worried he was.

The board wasn't gone more than fifteen minutes and Wolf had to wonder if that was good or bad. They all looked stern and disapproving when they came back in, so his money was on 'not so good'.

"Ladies and gentlemen." Commander Rahway settled with another sigh. "We understand that the dynamics of the 77th are necessarily not that of State Paranormal. It's not an ideal situation but this is what our politicians have given us. We also understand that you often encounter things in your city, for reasons unknown to this board, which are far beyond previously recorded paranormal events. Therefore, State rarely interferes. However, regulations are there for a reason."

She tapped her papers straight and folded her hands atop them again. "Officer Monroe, you will submit to further testing. The new developments regarding your rather odd talent are intriguing to say the least, and we are not pleased to be kept out of the loop."

Kyle sat forward as if he would protest, but he subsided and only said, "Yes, ma'am."

"Officer Gatling, when you are senior at a site, you are *senior*. You do not allow cult of personality or perceived experience to overrule your judgment."

Jeff swallowed hard. "Yes, ma'am."

"There will be a reprimand placed in your record in that regard." She searched the gloom for her next victim. "Officer Krisk."

Krisk gave a tail thump in acknowledgment.

The commander's exasperation ratcheted up a notch. "For all the gods' sakes, Krisk, please tell me there's someone who interprets for you."

With one scaly finger, Krisk pointed at Wolf.

"Well, thank Hecate for that." She shook her head. "Let the record show that Officer Krisk will be permitted an interpreter, his partner, Officer Alexander Wolf, if he is ever called before this board again.

"Officer Soren, please stand."

Slowly, Kash unfolded his long frame from his chair and went to stand at proper parade rest, hat tucked under his arm in the puddle of light by the desk.

"Officer Soren, your record with the Pittsburgh PD was exemplary. Commendations. Swift promotions. Never a single mark on your record. I understand that your reassignment may have been seen as a demotion and that you might harbor some resentment, no matter how well sublimated. But in matters of the arcane, we have experts here with years of experience. If you *ever* have a question regarding the safety of an inactive — yes, *inactive* — site again, you will place the call first. Our personnel will make the decision. And you will keep your rather impressive destructive powers locked away unless there is a clear, present and *immediate* danger that you are able to defuse."

"Yes, ma'am," Kash spoke calmly into the space she left for him.

"This is your first infraction of any kind, so we are inclined to be lenient. You are remanded to desk duty until further notice and we are placing you on a sixty-day probationary period. If I see so much as a whisper of your name come across my desk in conjunction with a broken regulation, I will have your badge. Do we understand each other?"

"Yes, ma'am." Now there was the tiniest quaver in Kash's voice, a hint of thickness, as if he tried to talk past a lump.

"Good. Out of my sight, all of you. Go behave like a proper department. We have two new officers to send you next week and I would appreciate it if they were not led astray by rogue officers who think they know everything."

Kash saluted, executed a perfect about face and stalked out without waiting for the rest of them as they scrambled and tumbled over each other to try to get out the door as fast as possible. *It could've been worse.* No one got fired. No one got reassigned. Really, it had gone just like Kash had wanted. Jeff had gotten a smack but Kash had taken the fall.

Wolf frowned, watching that too straight back several yards ahead of him. Sometimes getting what you wanted could still hurt a lot.

Chapter Two

Gold had just started to tip the leaves in Washington Park, careful bits of gilding from nature's best artists to hint at autumn's arrival while the days were still warm. Jason told himself he deserved a little poetic indulgence since he had the day off and some room to breathe. Would've been even better if his wolf had been off, too, but lunch in the park with Alex on such a beautiful day was a nice consolation prize.

He'd brought big juicy burgers for them both, with lettuce and tomatoes, of course, because vegetables, and Alex picked the spot. They settled on a bench down one of the main pathways, close enough to hear the fountain and see George standing perpetual guard at the tomb of the unknown Revolutionary War soldier, but not so close that the falling water would interfere with conversation or that tourists snapping photos would disturb them. Jason grinned. It was a very Alex kind of choice.

Sometimes Alex didn't say much. He could be happy watching people, dogs and squirrels, and they were comfortable enough together by now that they didn't need to fill the silences anymore. But Alex ate his burger in a deliberate, unfocused fashion instead of devouring it and his gaze was on the path in front of them instead of the life around them.

"Hey." Jason bumped shoulders with him. "What's wrong? I know yesterday wasn't fun but it's not still bothering you as much, is it?"

"It is." Alex chewed on the end of a fry, worrying at it instead of eating it. "I guess it really is. I get that everyone at State feels like they're better than us. We *are* the rejects. But how does it make sense to send your rejects to the biggest city in the state? Why does this state even have rejects?"

Jason waited. He guessed there was more as Alex frowned harder at the ground. Finally, he gave a little nudge with his elbow. "Alex?"

After three more fries vanished in slow increments, Alex said, "I don't get why they hate me so much."

The statement caught him so off-guard, Jason felt like he'd stumbled while sitting down. "Who could possibly hate you? Who are we talking about?"

"The werewolves." Sunlight glinted off the white threaded through Alex's dark hair as he shook his head. "I mean, it's not the first time I've run into it. The vamps don't like me, but I think that's mostly because I'm something weird."

"They've got a lot of room to talk."

"Weirder than them. But the weres? They *hate* me. I can smell it."

"Alex." Jason put a hand on his arm, little shivers telegraphing to him. "It's probably not personal. I don't know a thing about werewolves, but do they even like regular wolves?"

"Don't know. I guess I don't know anything about them either, really. Except the ones I've met are always assholes."

"Could be instinctive, you know. Territorial. They can't piss in the corners like they want to mark territory, so they're jerks to you instead."

"Maybe? I had an almost-scuffle with a vampire captain while I was there, too. But he calmed down quick. He wasn't *hateful* about it. He smelled vampy, not hatey."

"You should probably ask Carrington." Jason gave the hard forearm he was holding a final squeeze. He hated seeing Alex so upset, and he *was* upset, even though he was quiet and puzzled about it. "I bet he knows all about how things work in Harrisburg. Hey, I'm sorry they made you feel like crap."

"It's okay. I think they made all of us feel bad in different ways."

For a lot of guys, that would've been insightful. For Alex? It was in his wiring. He might not always understand why humans did things but he was tuned in to emotional currents better than most people were.

Jason pointed and tried for a stern expression. "You need to finish your lunch. Big guy like you needs his protein."

"You've been hanging out with Mom too much." Alex managed a smile and the little ache that Jason had been half-aware of eased around his heart. The hamburger met an honorable end as Alex devoured it in three bites, licking his fingers in a way that made Jason's face heat. "That was really good. Where did —"

The sudden frozen posture, index finger half-licked, might have been funny under other circumstances. Jason knew that look, though. *Crap.* "What is it?" he whispered.

"There's something here."

Jason bit back on the urge to say *I know that.* "What kind of something?"

Nostrils flared, head up, Alex sampled the air. "It's...like rabbit but not."

"Where?"

Alex stood slowly, turning toward a row of nearby bushes. "Over this way."

"When you say rabbit, babe, you don't mean dust bunnies, right?"

"No. Regular rabbit but wrong."

Helpful. Jason snorted but got up, preparing to follow.

"I don't know, all right?" Alex shot him a harried look. "I've never smelled anything like this."

"Sorry." Jason stayed two steps behind, letting Alex's senses lead them, ready to cut off whatever it was if there was a need to.

As they approached the hedge, Alex dropped to a crouch, making little whuffle-snorts like Jason's dogs did when they were on top of a particularly fascinating scent. Jason peeked over Alex's shoulder for a better look. In a miniature clearing between bushes, where the branches had been trimmed back, sat an animal that was twenty flavors of wrong.

He'd never seen a jackrabbit in person, but the body and hind legs were too long and the ears too enormous for this to be a garden variety bunny. That would've been strange enough, since no species of jackrabbit lived nearby and this looked like an Arizona jackrabbit with its radar dish, mostly naked ears. Jason could've accepted all that and put the animal's presence in the park down to being an escapee.

But he was with Alex, so why should the weird stop there? No, the worst bit was that this hare had horns. The animal science part of his brain suggested it could be *shope papilloma*, a nasty virus that caused horn-like tumors in rabbits and hares. He'd seen that in person, though, and those growths were irregular, ugly things. No, these horns had the smooth texture of natural horns, a full, proud rack growing between the huge ears.

"Jackalope," he whispered. *But those are hoax animals.* Someone was playing a weird prank. "Alex, do those horns look glued on to you?"

Alex shook his head, his pupils blown from the excitement of stalking. "No. We should catch it."

"We should try. It doesn't belong here. Hold tight." Jason backed off a few steps and put in a call to his department. "Julie? Hey. Yeah, I know it's my day off. Don't be a smartass. I was having lunch with Alex in Washington Park and we've got a non-native species here. Some kind of jackrabbit."

Maybe he should've mentioned the horns, but then Julie wouldn't have taken him seriously.

"She says hold tight. They're on the way." He took in the taut muscles in Alex's arms. His wolf was practically vibrating. "Alex, I know you're tempted. But we don't have the equipment."

A spare nod was all he got in response, Alex never taking his eyes off the thing-that-might-be-a-jackalope. A rustling in the bushes in front of them had the creature tensing, hunkered down as it prepared to use its powerful hind legs to spring away. A second jackalope made its way out of the bush and the first returned to unconcerned grazing. *Okay, if this is a joke, someone went to a* hell *of a lot of trouble.*

He was willing to bet David Attenborough and Steve Irwin had never had to deal with things like this.

Both antlered hares hopped out of the shrub clearing in favor of the nice manicured bit of lawn behind it. Jason signaled to Alex to circle around the other side of the lawn while he crept closer on the near side. They could at least attempt to keep the hares contained.

Alex kept well back, offering no threat, though Jason wondered what the critters would think if they caught his scent. The way dogs always reacted, he doubted that Alex's smell was fully human. It was yummy as far as Jason was concerned, but his nose wasn't that discerning.

Problem with parks? They were rarely empty. A mom with a stroller and a toddler walking alongside came up the path on Alex's side. The little guy stopped and pointed at the *funny bunnies* while Alex half-turned to speak to the mom, probably telling her to stay well back.

Mom wasn't the one worrying Jason. Her kid was way too focused on the animals. The toddler yanked away from his mom right on cue and ran out into the grass. Jason tensed, ready to run either way when the jackalopes fled, but the damn thing didn't act the way a legitimate hare would.

It charged. Head down, antlers first, the bigger jackalope hurtled at the kid.

Too far away to intervene, Jason yelled as he hurdled the shrubs, trying to startle the critter into changing directions. It didn't veer a single degree off course. Just to make things more fun, the smaller jackalope charged Jason. With no bag, no control pole, not even a cardboard box to put between him and those horns, he had no intention of engaging the animal. He dove to the side, but the thing was *fast*. The tines caught him in the side, sharp licks of flame along his ribs before he could roll away.

From his vantage point in the grass, he had a perfect view of Alex as he snatched the toddler up and met the larger jackalope's horns with the sole of his boot. He kicked it away, growling a warning at it. Not fair really, that Alex got to be handsome, heroic *and* a little dangerous.

The jackalopes fled, propelled through the park on their powerful hind legs. The kid seemed okay, scared rather than hurt as he clung limpet-tight to Alex. The mom was hysterical but she'd get over that. Jason rolled onto his back and found Julie peering down at him.

"Okay there, Shen?" she asked as she nudged at his ankle with her shoe. "What the hell were those?"

A rustle in the shrubs tugged Jason's head around. A flash of white flickered under the greenery. He thought he saw... No, that was about the dumbest thing ever. Too much excitement, probably.

"I'll live, Jules." He sighed as he say up and took in the damage. His poor Flyers T-shirt was a loss with three long rips where the horns had caught. "I don't even want to say 'cause you'll laugh at me. Damn city gets weirder every year."

"Tell me about it." Julie lifted her chin to indicate the park. "We'll do a quick sweep but I bet those whatever-they-were things are gone. You better get up unless you want your boy freaking out."

Yep. Alex had finished reassuring the mom and was striding across the grass, his mouth set in a grim line.

Jason resolved to start wearing darker T-shirts so blood wouldn't show. With a muffled groan, he heaved himself to his feet and dredged up a smile.

"Well, that was different. And not in a fun way."

Alex had his phone out. "You're bleeding."

"I kinda got that, big guy. I'm all right. If you start calling an ambulance, I'm taking that phone away."

"But—"

"No." Jason covered Alex's hand with his own. "I'm not spending five hours in an ER for scratches."

"Urgent Care." Alex poked a finger at Jason's chest. "I'll take you."

"Deal. But you get back to work once you've dropped me off."

Reluctantly, Alex returned his phone to his pocket. "And you'll call me when you're done."

Jason's eyelid twitched. "Alex. Hovering."

"Sorry." Alex sounded like he was choking on a growl. "That thing gored you. I thought... I was..."

"Worried. I know." Jason put a hand on his shoulder. "Hey. I'm okay. As antlers go, they were pretty small."

"Okay." Alex heaved a slow breath in and out. "Can I still drop you at Urgent Care?"

Blood was trickling into his waistband and the punctures were little pools of lava along his skin. Annoyed about being fussed at? Sure. Enough to be a macho asshole? No.

"Yeah. I'd appreciate that." He bumped shoulders with Alex as they made their way out of the park. "You were pretty amazing."

"I was?"

"You were. Damn, but you can *move*. Super Alex."

A blush climbed up from under Alex's collar. Jason was a little ashamed of himself that he tried for that blush sometimes. It was ridiculously cute on such a big guy.

"I was just—"

"Doing your job, Officer. I know. But I'm your boyfriend and I get to admire you while you do your job. That's how this works."

Even though Alex was bright red now, one of those deep, rumbly laughs got away from him. And for those? Jason would move small mountains.

* * * *

Wednesday evenings, Alex usually spent with his mom. Not that Wednesday. He showed up with Audacity on his shoulder, a grocery bag full of heavenly smells and a worried frown.

Jason took the bag from him and stole a quick kiss. "Hey. You should've called."

The frown deepened. "You told me not to call."

"I was asking you not to play mother hen. But coming all the way over here without calling? I could've gone out or something."

"Oh." Alex let out a breath that was half-huff, half-irritated sigh. "It's not that far."

"Not the point. And don't let your brain start spinning." Jason tugged him toward the kitchen. "Yes, I'm glad you're both here and thank you for bringing food."

The dogs danced and whined around Alex until he knelt down to pet and greet them. From his shoulder, Audacity patted each canine head that came in reach, as well. Genevieve and Race even got nose touches since they were both tall enough.

"You at least stopped at home first?" Jason took in the jeans and the obscure anime T-shirt.

"Yeah." Alex put Audacity down on the floor to explore. "I was... Mom said..."

Shaking his head, Jason came around the kitchen island and put his arms around Alex's waist to pull him close. "Hey, hey, what's all the nervous for? You know you can say whatever to me."

Alex's gaze couldn't settle, though he did snake an arm around Jason's uninjured side. "You were mad when I was...hovering. So I didn't call. But I was worried. Mom said I was making her nuts."

"Ha. She kicked you out."

"Yeah. Kind of." Alex nodded to the bag. "She packed food for us, though."

"*That's* why it smells so good." Jason abandoned his hold on his police officer to dive for the bag. "Oh, my God. She sent meatloaf. I love her meatloaf. *And* mashed potatoes." He opened the container to let the scent wrap around his head. "The kind she makes with cream cheese and garlic. Bless you, Miriam."

"You're so cute when you're all excited about food." Alex's tense-shouldered stance had finally relaxed and he managed a quirk of a smile.

"And I'm uncute when I'm not?"

Alex's frown was back, though his eyes sparkled. "This is what Mom calls *fishing*, isn't it?"

"Damn. Busted." Jason was about to ask a food-or-sex-first question when their stomachs let out synchronized growls. *Fair enough.* Sex on an empty stomach was overrated, anyway. Sometimes Alex liked both together, which was fine for, say, chocolate pudding, but would be disrespectful to Miriam's meatloaf.

They'd managed to get through second helpings and were both contemplating thirds when Alex started nuzzling. Not shocking that his nose led most sexual campaigns. Smells were powerful drivers of everything for Alex, from emotions to physical reactions. He licked at the side of Jason's neck, just a little swipe accompanied by a deep and unmistakably demanding growl.

Didn't mean Jason had to make things easy for him. "There's plenty more if you're still hungry."

Sharp teeth nipped at his earlobe. Alex pulled their stools closer together. "Not hungry," he breathed in Jason's ear.

"You kinda seem hungry still. We could go for ice cream?"

"Jason..." The growl rose in volume, sending a delicious shiver down Jason's back.

He turned and took Alex's face between his hands so he could pull that shaggy head around for a sweet, chaste kiss. "We're gonna have to move, big guy. You know how the fur-peeps get upset when we get going."

Alex grunted but didn't protest. Hecate in particular had barked frantically, which had set the others dogs off the last time they had tried getting hot and heavy in the kitchen. They'd had to stop when Race had started howling. Carefully disentangling himself, Alex slid off his kitchen stool and dumped what little food was left into one container.

"Good thinking," Jason said as he put their dishes in the sink to speed matters up. If they left any food out, certain critters would succumb to temptation and everything would end up on the floor. Besides, Jason had discovered after trial and error that Alex refused to leave a kitchen without cleaning up first. Helping was easier on both of them than trying to convince him to leave it until later.

In many ways, they were still navigating. Neither one of them had high mileage on their relationship odometers—new ground for both of them. But watching Alex as he strode to the stairway and shot Jason a smoldering look over his shoulder... Alex was something special. Scary strong and sometimes strange, sure. Also loyal, compassionate and open to everything going on around him. He was quiet because he liked to listen. He didn't talk endlessly about any one subject because he liked to learn.

He'd filled holes in Jason's heart that he hadn't known were there—cracks and chips from past failed relationships, arguments with family, casual nasty comments from strangers—small accumulations of hurts that didn't seem much day to day until someone came and soothed them, smoothed out the ragged edges, epoxied over the worst damage. They weren't *gone*. There was just such a sense of relief with Alex's repairs, like Jason hadn't realized he wasn't taking whole breaths before.

Damn straight he was going to try his best to make this work.

"You guys be good down here. Go take a nap." Jason petted four dog heads, then nearly tripped over three cats as he hurried upstairs. Audacity let out a questioning *mew* and Jason scooped her up to put her on the armchair with Tybalt. The huge tom curled around her, tucking her in close to his fluffy side. "We'll just be upstairs, little girl. Gives you a chance to visit."

By the time he got to the bedroom, Alex had already stripped. He stood in the middle of the carpet in all his hard-muscled, furry glory, arms crossed, erection at parade rest and coming to attention.

Jason leaned against the doorframe to admire the view. "Do people tell you all the time how gorgeous you are?"

"No. Most people are scared of me." Alex was doing his best to look stern and forbidding. A little twitch at one corner of his mouth betrayed him. "But thanks. Too much talk and too many clothes."

"Well, if you're gonna be bossy about it." Jason *tsked* and caught the hem of his T-shirt to yank it off. He managed half a yank when the material snagged the edge of his bandages. "Ow."

Immediately, Alex dropped all attempts at sexual play and hurried over to help him get untangled. "Are you okay?"

The worried frown was back and Jason wanted to bang his head against the door in exasperation.

"I'm sorry. Maybe we shouldn't be doing this."

"Yes, we should be doing this." Jason pulled in a breath, regretting the sharpness of his words. "I'm a little sore, babe. But I'm fine. So long as you don't want me turning cartwheels, no problem."

Alex wrapped an arm around him, carefully avoiding the bandages, and laid his head on Jason's shoulder with a sigh. "No cartwheels. I just feel bad."

"About what? You couldn't be in two places at once. More important to get the kid safe."

"Yeah." At least Alex snuggled closer. That was nice. "Just feel like you wouldn't have to deal with weird stuff if you weren't with me."

Jason ran his hands up and down that broad back, hoping to calm his Big Not-Really-Bad Wolf. "I'll take all the weird this city has to throw at me if I get you in the bargain, okay? I'd rather be there to help you when I can."

"So long as it's not *too* weird."

"We fought deadly evil sentient dust clouds together. Lagomorphs with horns are kinda normal after that."

He waited for Alex to ask what lagomorphs were but of course he didn't. Biologist parents. Instead, Alex started nuzzling at his throat and nosing behind his ear. Good. That was better. Jason backed up slowly, cupping Alex's gorgeous muscular butt in both hands to urge him along. His knees hit the bed sooner than he was expecting and he sat with a surprised *oomph*.

Alex heaved an exaggerated sigh and shook his head. "Still too many clothes."

"What? I met you halfway."

"Guess they won't take themselves off. So high maintenance."

Alex pushed with one shoulder to get Jason to lean back. A shiver ran through Alex's muscles as he popped the button and undid the fly of Jason's jeans. *Someone's excited.* A soft growl confirmed that as Alex yanked jeans and boxers all the way off in three sharp tugs. He didn't even give Jason a moment to breathe as Alex pushed him flat with one hand and spread his knees with the other.

Maybe it wasn't what he'd anticipated, flat on his back with his legs hanging off the edge of the bed, but he wasn't about to complain when Alex dove right in, nuzzling and snuffling at the crease of his thigh.

"Alex? Babe? Don't you want to —?"

"No."

Oh, god, the growl in Alex's deep voice made his balls ache.

"Not even —"

"Shh." Alex licked at the base of his cock, sending spark showers through Jason's groin.

He spread his knees farther and buried his fingers in Alex's thick hair, whispering, "Okay. Shutting up."

This was new. Not that he ever minded Alex's mildly aggressive moves during sex. Most of the time they started out wrestling, and even though it was playful, it got his blood boiling. But this took aggressive to a whole new level, almost too *possessive*. Was it anxiety-driven? Worry for him or even leftover adrenaline from the jackalope encounter? Jason pulled in a slow breath that caught on a strangled moan when Alex sucked on his balls. Nope, not the time to think about Alex ramping things up when the heat of his mouth and his agile tongue were making Jason melt into a puddle of electrified jelly.

Alex wrapped his fingers around Jason. That strong hand could stop a suspect in their tracks, but was so gentle as he rolled Jason's foreskin back. Squirming, Jason fought between wanting to watch and wanting to just flop back and feel. He ended up doing a little of both as Alex's tongue circled his tip. *God*, he was beautiful, the light from the streetlamp giving his skin a silver sheen and picking out the white in his hair.

Still growling, Alex wrapped his lips around Jason's cock and plunged down, holding him steady at the base and providing vacuum suction on his upstroke. Always careful of his sharp teeth, he let them make contact in little pinpricks as he eased his way up while Jason twitched and writhed at each lightning quick touch. He went slowly and the tender, precise attention snared him and dragged him toward the edge faster than any hard thrust and grunt of any kind with any other partner.

The constant vibration of Alex's growls didn't hurt one bit, either.

Gasping, both hands clutched in Alex's hair, Jason was about to make one last plea for a sixty-nine — "Alex! Oh, damn! *Alex!*" was all the warning he managed before his climax hit him like a dodgeball to the head. His cries were high-pitched and a little embarrassing but he didn't have room in his brain to worry about it with Alex turning him inside out with hard-suctioned pulls, drinking every last drop Jason had to give.

Jason's hands dropped to the bed. He lay there panting like the air in the room had thinned, staring at the ceiling until Alex's face hovered over him, grinning.

"Okay there?"

"Mmnph." Jason gave him a playful smack on the arm. "Wording. Forgot how."

Alex chuckled as he collapsed on his side next to Jason, fingers tracing lazy circles on his chest. "I don't mind not wording."

"Your turn." Jason poked at his chest and encountered something sticky. *Wait. He swallowed everything. This can't...* "Alex?"

"I, um. Yeah, I'm good."

"You...but I didn't even touch you." Jason ran a quick replay of whose hands had been where. "*You* didn't even touch you."

"Um." Alex rolled over on his back, rubbing both hands over his face. "It's your...when you get all worked up. Your scent. It, um, makes me a little...yeah."

Jason snickered. "It was so good, we both forgot how to word. My scent, huh? Wow. That's —"

"Weird?"

"Hot. Really, *really* hot."

Alex grunted and snuggled close to bury his face in the crook of Jason's neck. "But it's not human."

"It's not. But look, I know all the things and none of it freaks me out. Maybe that makes me weird, too. Don't care." Jason stroked Alex's back. "You staying?"

"Didn't bring a uniform."

"So you get up early."

Alex got an arm under Jason's legs and turned them so they were lying the right way round on the bed. "Okay. I—"

A thud came from the hall, followed by a plaintive *mew* and a tiny black paw thrust under the bedroom door.

Jason snickered. "Better let your daughter in before she tries to break the door down. Or learns how to open it."

"She will if you give her time." Alex heaved himself out of bed and opened the door. "We're right here. The houseful of playmates isn't good enough?"

Mrrr-iw.

"I see. But you don't sleep with me when Jason's at our house."

Mew.

"Right. Grandma's not here." Alex scooped her up. "Audacity wants to know if she can sleep with us."

"Of course she can. Most of the tribe sleeps up here in the winter, anyway. They'll probably stay downstairs tonight since it's still hot."

It wasn't late but Alex did seem tired. They snuggled in to spoon and Audacity claimed the space on top of the covers behind Alex's knees while Jason tried to get his brain to settle. His boyfriend talked to cats and had a nose as good as any bloodhound. Weird? No. More like extraordinary. Maybe Alex wasn't quite a superhero, but he was as close as anyone got outside the comic pages.

Chapter Three

Even though the squad room was never empty over the weekends, Monday mornings still had a certain feel to them, sort of a grumpy, vigilant quiet. Edgar the neon raven sulked on his perch, feathers fluffed and head tucked down low. Even Larry the coffee poltergeist's whistling was softer on Monday mornings as he went about making his undrinkable brew.

It didn't help that a forbidding cloud hovered over Kash's desk. He was his normal calm self on the outside, sipping his coffee and reading his emails, but Wolf could smell his anger simmering below the surface. Oh, he resented starting another week on desk duty, no matter how professional he was about it. While Kyle couldn't smell his partner's anger, he *lived* with Kash and probably didn't have to. He was abnormally silent — no teasing, no bad jokes — a shadow of their normal Kyle.

"Time, ladies, gentlemen and entities," Carrington called from his darkened corner of the squad room.

Everyone moved to secure computers and gather up mugs and cups before making their way to roll call. The lieutenant hadn't appeared yet that morning, though that wasn't unusual. Her office light seeped out from between her blinds, so they knew she was there. She would emerge exactly on the hour as she always did.

Wolf didn't rush, letting everyone go ahead of them. They stood toward the back of the room since Krisk hated the metal folding chairs in the assembly room. Who could blame him? There was nowhere to put his tail.

"Huh."

Krisk glanced over at him.

"Jason just texted. He said he's having a barbecue at his house tomorrow night and did I want to come."

Krisk frowned and waved a hand to ask for more information.

"It's, um, with his family."

With a huff, Krisk pulled out his phone to text.

You do not wish to engage with Jason's familial group

"Nervous about it, I guess." Wolf shook his head. "I mean, he says he never brings guys home. That they don't talk about him being gay. It just sounds...uncomfortable? Maybe even worse."

Data acquisition
Determine which familial elements are hostile

"Yeah." Wolf leaned against the back wall of the assembly room with a sigh. "That makes sense. Though that's rough. Going to a party to see who hates me."

Support for your chosen sexual partner
Addendum, reminder to inquire regarding foodstuffs to bring

"Oh, crud. Right. I need to ask." Wolf sent a quick text to Jason before silencing his phone for roll call. "Thanks for reminding me."

Krisk answered with a soft thump of his tail and lifted his chin, somehow managing to look smug. Tim was the last member of their mixed police and civilian force to arrive, and even though the little guy was an unidentifiable entity the size of a large caterpillar, Wolf was sure Tim thought of himself as an officer. He rolled up to the front row of chairs in his carefully constructed house transport ball of paper scraps, popped out of the top and squeak-announced his arrival. Jeff leaned over to converse with him and to straighten the tiny uniform hat on his fuzzy purple head.

The sharp silver scent of Lieutenant Dunfee reached Wolf a half-second before the martial click of her heels in the hall. He straightened from his slump, the humans in the room taking their cue from him as they claimed seats and halted conversations. Carrington remained slouched in his chair with his mirror shades on, but it was a bright morning and he probably still had a headache from the drive in.

Oddly, the lieutenant didn't smell quite like herself that morning. Wolf lifted his head, testing the air. Ah, someone was with her. Two someones? If he'd still had wolf ears, they would've been pricked forward in curiosity. Who would be sequestered in the lieutenant's office with her first thing in the morning?

He only had to wait a few seconds for the answer, so he didn't have time to get all worked up with anticipation. Lieutenant Dunfee swept in with her customary, "As you were." Two officers followed a step behind, both young, both in 77th uniforms, so Wolf figured they were the two transfers Commander Rahway had mentioned.

One was male, blond, an inch or two taller than Kyle, with skin almost as white as Carrington's. The other was female, as tall as Wolf, her black hair worn in four thick braids gathered into a ponytail. Both smelled nervous. Both had determined, serious expressions trying to mask that anxiety.

Two sets of eyes—one blue, one brown—widened when they caught sight of Krisk, and grew more shocked as they took in LJ and Hunter floating on one side of the room. The young man tripped and skittered sideways when he almost stepped on Tim's portable house. The young woman regarded Tim's peeped greeting with a dark frown.

The reaction was typical for people from State. Yes, they were used to the paranormal, but only *normal* paranormal. Wolf bit back a sigh and told himself not to prejudge. No matter what the lieutenant might have explained, the squad had still blindsided them. Didn't mean they were supernatural snobs.

"Good morning, everyone," the lieutenant began as soon as she gained the podium. "Yes, we have transfers. Keep your eyes in your heads and your questions to yourselves."

She continued on to roll call with deliberation, probably to give the new kids a chance to catch a couple of names, then propped her reading glasses on her nose and peered down at her papers.

"All right, regular patrol routes. I have no new updates for you this morning, though check the bulletins from State as always." She nodded to her left. "We have two transfers directly from Harrisburg today. From the cadet program. Officer Eva Dennis and Officer Jeremy Poole. Since this is their first assignment, I want them rotating through teams. We'll consider changes in partner assignments as it becomes necessary."

There were a couple of sounds of dismay and she glared over the top of her glasses. "Don't want to hear it. I'll make decisions for the best of the department. Later. For now—Officer Soren is our default desk sergeant. He'll draw up the rotation. For today, I want Poole starting with Gatling and Virago. Dennis with Wolf and Krisk."

"Throwing them in the deep end, ma'am?" Carrington drawled.

"Shut it, Loveless. Don't wear out my last nerve this early." She tapped her notes together. "Let's get to it, people. Remember, there's still an unsecured pair of, for want of a better word, jackalopes out there, so all necessary caution, please."

The young man, Poole, stared at her open-mouthed after the jackalope reminder. That one was going to have to adjust to a new level of weird fast or he was going to end up shell-shocked. Not Wolf's problem, though, and he was sure Jeff would try to ease him in gently. He didn't think he and Krisk were the best choice for someone's first day, but at least their rookie seemed better centered than the other one.

As the squad dispersed, Jeff hustled Jeremy Poole out, talking all the way, while Wolf made his way up front to Eva Dennis. He hesitated, then realized not shaking would be considered rude and offered his hand.

"I'm Officer Wolf. This is Officer Krisk."

Her hand didn't disappear in his like many human hands did and her handshake was firm without feeling like a challenge, though she still frowned. "Are you a werewolf, Officer Wolf? You sound like one."

"Ah, no. Not...no. I was a wolf. A curse made me human."

She nodded and turned her too-serious face to Krisk. "Are you cursed too, Officer Krisk? You were human once?"

Krisk shook her hand carefully, one brow ridge raised, his tail thumping.

"Um...no. Krisk is just...Krisk. And he understands but he doesn't speak human 'cause he doesn't have the right parts for it."

Eva stared at him in frank disbelief. "How do you work on cases together?"

"We text. And we're used to each other." Wolf pulled out his phone. "Um, probably should exchange phone info if you're riding with us."

"This better not be some weird come-on." Her frown grew darker.

Wolf cocked his head, trying to scent if she was truly angry. He was still getting nervous scent, so he went on, "I have a boyfriend. Krisk doesn't do...um...that. With humans."

"Does...? Never mind." Eva pulled out her phone and the three of them leaned close to exchange contacts.

"So..." Wolf cleared his throat as they made their way to the squad room. "Everyone here's good about personal stuff. And not asking. Except one thing. They'll ask what paranormal thing you do."

"Not a hell of a lot," Eva muttered with a snort. "What do you do? Besides being cursed."

"I don't do any psychic stuff but I kept some wolf." Wolf shrugged. He was used to the question. "Better senses. Better hunting instincts. Stronger and faster than a human my size. Krisk is like me, only bigger."

"And a damn lizard," Eva said under her breath. Maybe she thought they couldn't hear her. Humans often underestimated just how good *better* hearing was.

"Every other officer has a psychic thing. Okay, not Carrington."

"Loveless? The vamp?" She stopped them with a hand on Wolf's arm at the squad room's entrance. Bitterness colored her voice as she said, "I thought all the officers here were rejects."

"Needs special blood. The other vamps don't think he's a real vamp."

"Oh." Eva's mouth twisted, her throat working as she tried to get some emotion under control. "I...see auras."

Wolf matched her frown. "All the time? That doesn't sound fun."

"No. I have to concentrate. When I get them, they're *stupid* auras."

"They're..." Wolf turned that around a few times. "I don't understand."

"You know the picture emojis you have on your phone? That's sort of what I see. A bunch of little pictures dancing around someone." Eva squinted at Wolf. "Yours are puppies and kittens and cute woodland creatures. And books. Which, if I didn't know you were a cop, I'd think you were a Disney princess."

"Oh. So auras that don't tell you anything useful?"

"Pretty much."

"And Jeremy?"

Eva managed her first crooked smile. "He levitates."

Wolf waited for more but finally asked. "That sounds like a normal thing?"

"Badly." Eva called across the room to her fellow rookie. "Jer, might as well show them. They're already asking."

"Aw, man." Jeremy's shoulders slumped. "Can't we be normal for one day?"

Vikash leaned against the nearest desk and gestured with his coffee cup. "You're normal here, Jeremy. No matter how your abilities manifest. We're paranormally atypical, not broken."

"You say that now." Jeremy heaved a sigh. "Okay. I should have a little space. Please."

Hunter popped up from under Wolf's desk with Audacity perched on her sleeves, presumably having let the kitten out of her carrier so they both could watch. When Eva frowned in their direction, Wolf concluded that some of her frowns were thinking rather than unhappy ones.

"There's a kitten."

"I'll explain in a minute," Wolf whispered as Jeremy squeezed his eyes shut and appeared to be holding his breath.

An electric crackle zipped through the air. Jeremy let out a slow breath and rose six inches from the ground. It all went so well at first that Wolf wondered if Eva had been teasing him. Then Jeremy tipped, cursing and flailing as his feet replaced where his head had been. A desperate grab for a desk edge sent him careening sideways, still upside-down, until he bounced off the far wall and finally ran out of momentum, hovering eight feet off the floor in an uncomfortable sideways-tilted position.

"Little help? Please?" Jeremy's words were tired and resigned, and more than one officer looked ashamed to have failed to stop the demonstration.

Krisk stomped over and reached up, the only one of them tall enough to manage without standing on a chair. Careful where he put his claws, he took Jeremy by the wrist and gently pulled him down.

"So you can't come back down?" Amanda asked what they were all thinking.

Jeremy shrugged as he regained his feet in Krisk's strange and awkward embrace. "I *can*. Usually end up dropping myself on my head."

"Certainly not the strangest thing we've had in the squad room," Carrington offered.

There were nods all around and Shira added, "Or anywhere close to the most dangerous."

Jeremy's shoulders slumped, though he still eyed them all warily. "Thanks. I guess we kinda got too used to being the weird in the room."

"*I* never got used to it," Eva protested, then shrugged. "The instructors at State were so damn sure they could teach us to be *useful*. *Normal*. Yeah. That worked."

"And now we're here." Jeremy swallowed hard, staring at his shoes.

Carrington made his way across the room slowly, one foot in front of the other, a predator's stalk. He stopped in front of Jeremy, arms crossed over his chest. The poor boy stumbled back a step. Who could blame him?

"And now you're here," Carrington said in his gentlest tone. "Where you will find that even small, unidentifiable oblongs of purple fluff are useful."

Tim chirruped at that, straightening proudly atop his paper house.

Beside Wolf, Eva let out the breath she'd been holding. "Okay." The sharp scent of her anxious, brittle anger faded. She raised a dark eyebrow as they walked to Wolf's desk. "Now. About the kitten…"

Chapter Four

Wolf shifted the container with the chocolate cake to one arm so he could kiss his mom's cheek and rub faces with Audacity. "I don't think I'll be too late." He hefted the cake saver toward her. "And thanks for this."

"You should be proud of that, Alex." Mom patted his chest. "I just supervised."

Maybe it was dumb, but he *was* proud of having made a cake to bring to Jason's barbecue, icing and all, from scratch. He couldn't have done it without Mom's direction. Still, he'd done it and had realized he *enjoyed* baking in the process. Sure, he'd fetched and carried for Mom plenty of times when she baked, but it was always different, wasn't it? Doing something—a *human* thing—with his own hands.

For the rest? He wanted to see Jason, of course, but he didn't really want to go. He would be the only outsider there at a family gathering. Even the other in-laws and significant others had the advantage of knowing each other. So Jason said. Maybe some of them hated each other. Maybe some of them would hate him.

But he hadn't thought to ask who got along with whom and would be walking in blind. For someone like Jason, it wouldn't be a problem. He could talk to anyone and it would never be weird or uncomfortable. For Wolf? Every new human acquaintance was a potential minefield of social disaster.

When he turned to wave at his mom, Audacity lifted a paw to bat the air in what could have been mistaken for a wave in return. Silly, to assign human gestures to a kitten. Though... She had seemed to understand that she was to stay with Grandma this evening and let him leave for Jason's without a fuss.

I don't want to do this. I could call and say... What? Lie? No, he couldn't do that, but if he told Jason the truth, that he didn't want to meet his family? That might be worse. He told himself to stop being such a scared cub and started the car. *Go see Jason. Meet his pack. If it's really bad, don't stay too long.*

Pack. That was half the problem. Entering pack space as an outsider was always nerve rattling. The other half was something Jason had said when asked if he was out to his family. *We don't talk about it.* So, would Wolf just be a *friend* this evening? Could he go along with something that would be a half-truth?

He jumped in his seat when a car's horn blared behind him. The light had changed. This was stupid, thinking so hard that he lost track of his surroundings. Dangerous. He growled at himself. Whatever happened, happened, and there wasn't any use worrying at it like a leftover thigh bone.

Jason had said to come any time after six and it was still a quarter to when Wolf turned onto his street. He thought he'd be early enough to have a few minutes with Jason and to help set up, but the street in front of Jason's house was crammed with cars large and small. He found a spot several houses down and tried to wrestle down his disappointment. Jason's family didn't believe in fashionably late. He meandered past a Mercedes, a Lexus, a minivan on steroids and a Porsche before he got to the front walk, every vehicle another ping on his fish-out-of-water-in-a-desert-landscape meter.

His steps faltered as he neared the door. There were a *lot* of people in there. Wolf squared his shoulders, opened the screen and walked in. Conversation in the living room ceased, what seemed like dozens of eyes pinning him where he stood.

"Um…hello," he croaked out. "I'm Alex."

The disorientation of walking into a full room settled on eight pairs of eyes, not dozens, some curious but guarded, at least two openly hostile. He fidgeted, face heating, unable to think of a single appropriate thing to say since no one had answered. The oldest man in the room leaned forward to speak in Mandarin to one closer to Jason's age. That one answered. They both laughed.

Yeah…this is going great.

One of the women with echoes of Jason in her features glared at the men and leaped up from her place on the sofa, stepping over legs and the coffee table to get to Wolf.

"I'm Lisa." She hooked her arm through his and steered him toward the kitchen. "Good to meet you." When they reached the little hallway between rooms, she whispered, "Don't pay any attention. Dad doesn't like anyone new. *Jason's* going to be glad you're here."

"Thank you," Wolf murmured as he tried to remember who *Lisa* was. His rattled brain finally latched on—the oldest sister, only a year younger than Jason.

While Jason didn't talk about family much, he had mentioned this sister—the biologist, his companion in all things good and bad when they were little. She was married—maybe? He had to wonder which one of those unwelcoming faces had been her husband.

The kitchen was better, with two unfriendly gazes falling on him instead of several—one older woman and one ancient woman—and Jason.

"Alex, you made it!" Jason hurried over and took the cake saver from him. *Alex*, without endearments, but with a quirked smile and something that might have been an apology in his eyes. "What's in here?"

"Chocolate cake," Wolf couldn't get his voice above a murmur, the unwavering scrutiny too much for him.

"Ha! My favorite." Jason leaned in and hesitated. Then something hardened in his eyes and he finished the gesture to kiss Wolf's cheek. "Thank you."

A disgruntled sound came from one of the women. Lisa gave them a wry smile. But now that Wolf had accomplished the one definite thing he had to do, he stepped back, empty-handed and uncomfortable.

"Um... Can I...help? With stuff?"

The tiny ancient woman snorted and said something short and sharp in Mandarin to the other woman, probably Jason's mom. She said something equally sharp back, glaring daggers at him. He knew a word here and there from Jason but couldn't follow, though he heard *gwai lo* more than once.

"*Nai nai.*" Jason turned with a soft hiss of disapproval and opened the refrigerator. With a little shake of his head, he pulled two huge bowls and a tray off the second shelf and handed the bowls to Wolf. "Thanks, Alex. Come on out with me and we'll get things on the grill."

Wolf nodded, mute and unhappy, and tried to make himself small as he padded outside. Not that he'd come with any illusions. He'd known there wouldn't be magical acceptance. Knowing didn't make it easier. This was Jason's pack, whom he loved with all his considerable heart. Wolf didn't expect them to love him, but what if they never got around to liking him? Someday, Jason might feel that he had to choose. If he chose pack, Wolf wouldn't blame him, wouldn't be angry, but his heart would break.

* * * *

"Please stop, *Nai nai*," Jason begged his grandmother before he followed. "He doesn't know the words, but he senses things without them."

"Then he *is* a demon," she said stubbornly and went back to chopping daikon.

The dogs had already mobbed Alex by the time he got outside, the kids hanging back with the wary, solemn gazes of half-wild creatures. Jason set his tray beside the grill and crouched down with the dogs, getting a face full of Genevieve's tongue. Bad enough that he was the family disappointment — he was used to the verbal barbs — but anger had started a slow simmer down below at the hurt on Alex's face.

He pushed the greyhound away gently. "Alex, you okay? Was my grandma too much?"

"I —" Alex's mouth twisted as he looked up at the sky, blinking hard. "She — your grandma. I...I sort of understand her. She was angry. I'm…a stranger. And strange. She was just angry. Not like in the front room."

The front room? God damn *it.* "What did they say to you?"

"I don't…know. It just didn't feel, um, friendly."

"Those jerks." Jason knew who the likely culprits were. His dad and his brother Paul, probably. And damn them, if Alex broke down in tears, which seemed imminent, he was going to let them have it, family or not. "I'm sorry, hon."

Alex nodded, hiccoughing a breath and swiping at his eyes. He managed a crooked smile when little Hecate tried to climb him, though. The dogs knew he needed them. "I'm okay. I guess I expected something like that? But wasn't ready? Lisa was nice."

"She better be nice to you or I'll kick her butt." Jason leaned their foreheads together, tangling his fingers in Alex's hair and shaking gently. "If it gets too much, you don't have to stay, all right?"

"All right." Alex hauled in a long breath, pulling himself together. "What's *gwai lo*?"

"*Gweilo*. It's a…" *Racial slur. Insult.* "Not a nice way to refer to foreigners. Westerners."

"Oh." Alex pulled back, blinking. "Is that the problem? Not that I'm a…male?"

Jason smoothed Alex's hair as he stood up. "For my *nai nai*? Probably. She's old fashioned and got angry when Anna started seeing Ken, since he's Korean. For the rest? They'll just need to get over it."

Not that Dad, Mom or even Paul would get over it any time soon. *What have I dragged you in to, Alex?* It had felt so brave when he'd asked Alex to meet the family. Now he just felt like a coward, not taking a firmer stand right away. But you didn't make waves in the family.

You didn't humiliate your parents by calling them on their prejudices where everyone could hear.

Something tugged at his T-shirt as he opened the hood of the grill to check the coals. "Uncle Jason?"

He turned to find one of Lisa's twins at his elbow. "Yes, Jenny?"

"Who's that?" She didn't point. At seven, she was old enough to know it was rude. Instead, she nodded toward Alex.

Don't be a coward. He swallowed hard and didn't dissemble. "That's my boyfriend, Alex."

"Oh. He's big. Can he help us get the beanbag game set up?"

Jason gaped at her a moment, wondering if his brains were leaking out his ears. *That's...it?* "Well, ah, you should probably ask him, don't you think?"

After a short consultation, which included Jenny making sure that Alex knew the names of *all* the animals in Uncle Jason's house, she took him by the hand and led him to the shed at the back of the garden where the games were stored. The rest of the kids – her twin, Tyler, and Paul's three little ones ranging in age from six to three – all trooped after, watching in awe as Alex retrieved the board in one smooth motion from its shelf near the ceiling of the shed. Not that it was *that* heavy, but the kids were used to needing two grownups to wrestle it down.

The leaden stone lifted from Jason's chest. With the kids, Alex smiled and laughed, patiently setting up and sorting out how they would play. The kids didn't care that Mr. Alex was seeing Uncle Jason and they reacted to him as most kids seemed to, with near immediate trust and inclusion.

My boyfriend, the kid magnet. Jason chuckled as he started to pile meat and veggies on the grill.

Hostilities weren't limited to Alex that evening, though. Mom and his youngest brother, Daniel, engaged in a short, spectacular argument when he arrived on his motorcycle with his latest girlfriend. Astrid was tall, blonde and very white. To say Mom disapproved would have been like saying I-76 was a teensy bit busy at rush hour. Jason felt guilty for thinking it, but he was glad the argument had taken attention off Alex.

Lisa and Julia came out a few minutes later, carrying more food for the table. In birth order, Lisa was second and Julia fifth, but Julia had always seemed older than all of them. A dance instructor, she lived alone, didn't date, and though she was hounded about marriage and children by parents, grandmother and aunts at every family gathering, she was serenely content with her life. Lisa, on the other hand, was the perfect daughter — successful, married to a traditional Han husband, children — but not anywhere near so serene.

"Awfully handsome." Julia hip-bumped her sister. "You think Jason bribes Alex to go out with him?"

Lisa gave a sage nod. "Probably. Or he might have a thing for short, squat men."

"Hey!" Jason brandished the spatula at them. "I'm right here."

"Oh, no! We didn't see you there," Julia said with feigned shock, though the mischief drained from her eyes. "I'm sorry they were nasty to Alex."

"I should've planned it better instead of letting him run the gauntlet like that." Jason shook his head as he basted shrimp and turned vegetable skewers. "Thanks, Lis, for the rescue."

"He's so cute, I couldn't just let them snark at him." Lisa laughed as she watched the beanbag game, Alex lifting toddler Luke so he could drop his beanbag in the highest cut out on the tilted board. "Good with dogs. Good with kids. I might steal him."

"You'd have to let him sniff you first."

"You're not going to explain that, are you?"

"Nope."

Before long, Dan and Astrid joined them on the patio and Alex ambled over, surrounded by a gleeful horde of kids and dogs, to ask what the little ones could have to drink. Alex relaxed when introductions didn't include handshakes and conversation was friendly if superficial, until the rest of the family trooped out for dinner.

Jason finagled it so Alex sat between him and Julia at the picnic table, with Lisa across from them. The kids sat at their own miniature picnic table and ate just about enough to keep a pair of depressed sparrows alive before they escaped to go play again. Completely expected and the adults didn't intervene too much. What was unexpected was that despite some of Alex's favorites to tempt him—hamburgers, dan dan mian, hui guo rou, barbecued shrimp—he barely ate more than the kids. He kept his head down, obviously unwilling to test the conversational waters again with the older relatives at the table.

"So. You're a police officer?" Mama asked sharply.

Jason had to nudge him before Alex realized he was being addressed. "Yes, ma'am."

"This district?"

"No, ma'am. I'm, um…" Alex swallowed hard. "Assigned to a special unit. City wide."

Jason shot his mother a look, *please stop*, but she was relentless. "What does this special unit do?"

"It's police work, Mama," Julia said softly. "Alex might not be able to talk about it."

"Of course he can talk about it." Mama waved her fork at Jason. "I'm sure he talks to —"

A child's terrified scream cut her short. Alex was up and racing for the kids before anyone else could move. A strange shape strafed the huddled pack of nieces and nephews as Jason watched in horror. A bird? But that quick glimpse had revealed a silver sheen covering it. Some new kind of drone? Jason hurried over to see if there was any real danger.

The kids were in a tight, frightened knot, shielded by Alex's bulk as a second silver thing streaked toward them. Close enough to reach, Jason tried to grab hold of it but it slid through his fingers, leaving an unpleasant oily residue behind. He had a quick glimpse of stubby wings and a beak reminiscent of a pelican's before it vanished into the trees again. Despite his failure, or maybe because of it, the other male members of his family tried to catch the things as they continued to swoop and dive for the children.

They all failed just as miserably as Jason had.

Lisa and Anna had the kids now, trying to keep their heads protected and edge them back to the house. Alex straightened as he whipped off his T-shirt and got Julia to give him the long-sleeved button-down she wore over her tank top.

"Jason." He pointed to the old maple in the corner of the property, all his nerves evaporating in the face of Emergency Alex Mode. "Up there. Start throwing things at them. Get them to come at us."

"Don't antagonize them, you idiots!" Paul shouted, red-faced and panting from failing to catch the things.

"Who's the animal control officer? You?" Julia said with arched brows.

Ignoring them both, Jason started to chuck beanbags at any rustling maple leaf. His third beanbag hit something behind the foliage with a wet *thunk*, followed by a strange warbling cry. A streak of silver hurtled from the branches, heading straight for him. Before he could even duck, a snarl came from his right and Alex leapt for the thing, snaring it in his T-shirt and forcing it to the ground. He had it tied in a neat bundle and sprang back to his feet while everyone gaped at him.

Jason could've sworn he heard more than one of his sisters let out wistful, admiring sighs.

"Daniel! Go grab a couple of cat carriers from the front closet!" Jason called out before he began his barrage on the tree again.

Alex kept his gaze locked on the leaves, weight shifted forward. Oddly, his muscles weren't tense. He stood ready but loose and relaxed — to Jason's eyes, more focused, more *present* than before. The second silver thing burst from cover, again arrowing right for Jason. Alex exploded from his half-crouch, leaping sideways for a spectacular flying tackle as he caught the thing in Julia's shirt.

Shoulder to shoulder, he helped Jason wrestle the odd beasties into the carriers and retrieve the shirts. Now that they weren't zipping around like ungainly dragonflies, he could make out that they were animals and not machines as they waddled about in their containers, clacking their oily silver beaks and making unhappy trilling sounds.

"I'm sorry," Alex told Julia as he returned her shirt. "It probably needs a wash now. Those, um, bird things are covered in something slippery."

"Not a problem, Officer Wolf." Julia gave him a wry grin. "Worth the price of admission."

Alex flushed from the roots of his hair to halfway down his chest, making a futile effort to cover himself with his balled up, slimed T-shirt. And honestly? Jason wasn't too happy with all those eyes staring at his Alex, either.

"Alex, hon, you want to go inside and call it in where it's quieter? Maybe grab one of your shirts from upstairs?"

Maybe that had been a little too much territorial information there, not only acknowledging their relationship where everyone could hear but also making it clear that Alex kept clothes in the house. Jason would hear about it later.

Jason spent a few minutes making sure the kids were okay, then a few more herding them away from the carriers after they'd gotten over their scare and wanted to see the *weird birds*, as Jenny put it. When the squad car from the 77th pulled up, he was surprised to see Carrington and Amanda on such bright day, and that they had a third officer with them, a young woman who was almost as tall as Alex, who had gone out front to brief them. She was squinting at people as she came into the backyard and gave Paul a wide berth.

"Afternoon, everyone. I'm Officer Loveless, these are Officers Zacchini and Dennis." Carrington gave the gathering a cordial nod. "Jason, good to see you. Are these the entities?"

Jason moved over as Carrington crouched beside him to peer into the front of one of the cat carriers. "Afraid so. They could be something natural we've never seen, I guess. But I have doubts there."

Carrington removed his mirror shades for a better look. "Interesting. Are the children unharmed?"

"Everyone's fine. Alex caught them pretty fast."

"Well done, Officer Wolf." Carrington patted Alex's leg and veered a step sideways when he stood again.

Officer Dennis unexpectedly beat Amanda there with her hand under Carrington's elbow. "You *sure* you don't want an umbrella, at least? The sun's still so bright."

"Quite annoying. Most likely have a headache later," Carrington muttered as he shoved his shades back on. "Ladies and gentlemen, if you would kindly remain here in the garden, these officers will take your statements."

Officer Dennis was still staring at the department's vampire, open-mouthed. Amanda nudged her with an elbow. "You get used to it, kid. He's not the garden variety vamp."

"Jason, Wolf, if you would, please." Carrington motioned them toward the house and followed them into the kitchen.

"New assignment?" Jason asked as he snagged waters for them from the fridge.

"We received two rookies this week. Thank you." Carrington swept off his hat and looked like he wanted to slump face first onto the table. "Was a little bright out there. Nice kids but they have a bit to learn. So, any ideas what we have here? Any warning before the attack?"

Alex stared at the floor, arms crossed over his chest. "I was...distracted. Didn't notice anything.

Those…birds. I guess they're birds. They don't smell like much though."

"Hey." Jason balled up a napkin and threw it at him. "You kept the kids safe. You caught the things. Don't get all guilty here."

"Hmm. I'd like us to be sure. Wolf, would you mind going out there and having a sniff around where the entities were?"

Jaw clenched tight enough that Jason wondered if they would hear cracking teeth, Alex nodded and strode back outside.

Once the door closed behind him, Carrington asked softly, "Is he all right?"

"Mostly. My mom was interrogating him before the attack." Jason tamped down on the urge to say that his family had been pretty horrid. Not relevant or any of Carrington's business.

Carrington shuddered. "I completely understand about how unnerving mothers can be. Any opinions, since you're the animal expert?"

"I got nothing. Thought it might be a bird that came into contact with a chemical spill. It feels…oily? Greasy? It's not oil, though. I know what that looks like on a bird. This looks metallic and damned if it doesn't look like it's *part* of the bird."

"Curiouser and curiouser," Carrington murmured. "Would you mind terribly if we borrowed Wolf when we take the entities in?"

"Thanks for asking, but saying no would feel like interfering in police business." Jason let out a wry chuckle. "It's all right, Carr, really. I get it." *I'll put his cake in the fridge and save it for later. Just for us.*

* * * *

72

Two hours later, after Alex had offered up the earnest promise that he would return or replace the cat carriers and had gone with the squad car, Jason was finishing the cleaning up in the kitchen with his mother. She worked efficiently as always, but in complete silence. No picking at how he organized his kitchen, no cataloguing his lack of a good spice cabinet, no poking at his eating habits.

"Mama, you haven't smiled all day." Probably not the right opening line. Jason cringed as soon as he said it.

"I thought he was just another police officer," she spat out. "Another *white* policeman. But no. We all watched. He's some hero out of stories. Not fully *human*."

Jason watched her stiff back as she scrubbed furiously at the counters. "I know, Mama. I...know what he is."

"Do you? When *Nai Nai* called him *gweilo*, I thought she meant his skin. I think she knew and meant it in the older sense. Demon. Something powerful and more than natural."

"He's...there's nothing evil about him, Mama. But I can't argue that he's a hero. Almost a demigod sometimes."

She jerked around to glare at him. "Bad enough that you make your life hard by choosing to be *that* way. But this? I see how you look at him with your heart flopped at his feet. But he won't stay. He needs someone like him. Maybe if you'd tried harder with your life. Made something of yourself."

He couldn't find anything to say to that and settled for tying off the near-to-bursting garbage bag to take out. Once outside, he stopped to watch the rising moon. Beautiful, untouchable, the moon took no notice of him, of course. He disagreed with his mother about so many things, but this evening she was right. He wasn't anything special and eventually, Alex would see that too.

Chapter Five

"You figure it out yet?" Amanda stopped by Wolf's desk the next morning after roll call.

Wolf shook his head. "Not yet. It's...the scent... It's on the tip of my tongue."

"You mean on the tip of your nose," Kyle said with a snicker.

The previous evening, Wolf had returned to the squad room to help secure the strange birds and to give a full statement. Carrington had insisted on a catalog of scents Wolf had picked up and as he started naming the ones he could, he'd realized that he'd smelled the same unidentifiable thing at the jackalope sighting. It was making him crazy, but he couldn't figure out what it was. Something that was dusty, but more than dust. Not a direction he wanted to think in, since that brought on memories of feral dust bunnies.

What he'd wanted to do was go home and crawl into Jason's arms. To try to banish the images of hostile, angry eyes glaring at him. Even after he'd taken down the bird things, most of Jason's family had still stared at him. Some of them, like Jason's parents and his brother Paul, had been even angrier. Oh, yes, it worried him and had cost him sleep. He wasn't giving up yet, but what if Jason's family never gave up either? What if they always rejected him and Jason was forced to choose? Wolf's stomach turned uneasily as he tried to concentrate on work.

"It'll come to me. Don't have it yet."

"We need to send this up the line." Vikash said it calmly but with wary deliberation. "Since we have a connection between the two sightings. State will want to know."

Carrington's eyebrows rose. "It's a bit early to be talking about connections."

"Please, Carr. For my peace of mind." Vikash went back to sipping his coffee for a few moments. While staring at his screen, he said, "Woofen-poofs."

"I know you're kinda mad at them, Kash. But *that* doesn't sound like a nice thing to call the people at State." Kyle gave his partner a puzzled frown.

"What? Oh." Vikash waved Wolf and Carrington over to his monitor. "No. The captured entities. I've found them."

The screen showed a picture of a vaguely pelican shaped bird with stubby wings, one that appeared to be made out of metal. The article's header read *Woofen-poofs*. Like the jackalopes, they were hoax animals, and like the jackalopes, had been made up as a joke. Wolf didn't find the things in the holding room terribly funny.

"Well. And so you did," Carrington murmured. "Kash, whatever led you to this?"

"Looking up the jackalopes. Other hoax animals came up. Wikipedia has its uses."

Carrington patted his shoulder. "Well done. Now when I make the call to State, they'll be sure to think I've lost my mind."

Hard to say if they did, but Carrington was on the phone to Harrisburg for more than half an hour. It sounded like he was being passed up the chain of command, since he had to repeat the story more than once. When he finally hung up, his expression had soured.

"They're sending an *advisor*."

"Guess they don't trust us to handle shit on our own now." Vance huffed as he plunked down at his desk.

"We will give the advisor every consideration and our full cooperation." Carrington stood from his desk so he could meet everyone's eyes in the squad room, or the general vicinity of eyes in some entities' cases. "LJ, Hunter, no nonsense. Edgar, I swear if you cuss at them, I will pluck you and fry you."

Edgar let out an offended squawk but surprisingly refrained from any curse words.

"This is either babysitting or spying. Either way, we need to be at our best."

"When are they coming?" Jeff asked as he chewed on a nail.

Nervous became the overwhelming odor in the squad room.

A paperweight leaped off Shira's desk as she asked, "And do we know who?"

"I don't know who yet. Most likely this afternoon." Carrington sighed. "It was lovely not seeing any of them all this time."

Amanda patted his shoulder on the way past. "Professional's a two-way street, Carr. They better not start shit either."

Carrington didn't look comforted. Out of all of them, he might have had the hardest time at State Paranormal. Wolf wouldn't have done much better, but he'd never been assigned there. Carrington had and the regular vamps had been relentlessly cruel to him, which didn't give Wolf a high opinion of them. What he'd seen during his last visit to State hadn't helped.

* * * *

When Wolf and Krisk came back from patrol after four, a van with the State Paranormal shield was just pulling into the parking lot. Four officers in crisp black uniforms leaped out and hurried to open the back doors. Two jumped into the rear of the panel van and two stayed outside to help pull out a gurney. At first, Wolf was thoroughly confused since he thought it was a stretcher. Why would they bring an injured officer here? But no, what sat atop the gurney was a white box, about seven feet long... *Looks like a coffin.*

As disturbed as he was curious, Wolf jogged up the stairs to hold the door open for the State contingent, who hustled their burden through the door without so much as a thank you. Krisk slammed his tail on the steps, his meaning quite clear.

"Yeah. Rude," Wolf agreed as they trailed inside.

The squad room was nearly empty, officers just starting to trickle in from afternoon patrols. Vikash was there, of course, rising slowly from his desk. Amanda was in the back corner, so Carr had to be somewhere. Audacity stood on Wolf's desk chair, tiny paws up on the desk as if that were *her* workstation. She mewed when she saw Wolf, but he motioned for her to stay put.

Damn it. Should have had LJ take her out of the squad room for the afternoon.

The State officers locked the wheels on the gurney and the one at the head rapped politely on the box's lid. Snicks came from inside as if someone was undoing latches and the lid eased open. The officers in black scrambled to help lift, revealing an interior of quilted padding in a dark red. The occupant sat up, blinking at the squad room lights, and allowed the officers to help him down. Male, yes, definitely. Vampire, without a doubt. When the State officers backed off, it was Wolf's turn to blink. Blond hair pulled back in a neat tail, gray eyes sweeping the room, their guest wasn't just any vamp. It was Captain Valbuena.

"Captain." Vikash came forward to offer a handshake. "Good to have you here."

The delivery was flawlessly professional, but Wolf picked up the clipped, unhappy undertone.

"Officer Soren," the vamp captain's greeting was cool and cautious. "I was given to understand you were on administrative leave?"

"No, sir. Desk duty."

Just a hint of patronizing smile got through the frost. "Ah. My mistake. The board was lenient."

Wolf didn't wait to listen to any more stilted greetings. He hustled toward the back of the building, looking for Carrington. He was, as State had pounded into their heads, their senior officer. He didn't have to search long. Carrington was in the break room, drinking an afternoon snack.

"Wolf? Whatever's the matter? Your heart's going at an unsafe speed."

"I really didn't need to know you can hear my heart from there." Wolf pulled in a deep breath. "Officers from State are here. They sent Valbuena. In a box."

It shouldn't have been possible with his complexion, but Carrington paled. He rose slowly with both hands gripping the table. "They sent the *Colonel*? That bigoted, high-handed bastard?"

"Um...no? Captain Valbuena, not Colonel."

"Ah." Carrington stood there sipping at his blood snack, staring at the table. "He's not as bad. Still, odd that they'd send a vampire."

"Yeah. It was...the transport... Just too weird." Wolf shook his head. "Are they brothers or something? The Valbuenas? I figured they must be related."

Carrington gave him a sideways glance, searching for something he obviously didn't find since his hunched shoulders relaxed. "Ah, no. It's an old-fashioned vampire custom, not strictly adhered to any longer. So it dates them a bit."

"What does?"

"Colonel Valbuena is Richard's sire. He, ah...you do know the term?"

"Yeah." Wolf nodded. "I know that one."

"Good. Because of this, Richard took the Colonel's last name when he was turned. It used to be expected, a sort of discarding of the old life and taking up the new. But that happens less and less these days, now that vampires can be contributing members of society."

"It's why you kept yours?"

Carrington finished his snack and tucked the cup back into his insulated lunch bag. "My dear Wolf, I wouldn't have taken that miscreant's name even if it had been a hundred years ago. He left me to die in front of the ER doors. Yes, he turned me but I'd never call him *sire*."

"Yeah." Wolf cut off the protective growl that had started in his chest. "I get that."

"Hmm, yes." Carrington patted his shoulder with a weary smile. "Of all people, I imagine you do."

By the time they made their way back out to the squad room, Lieutenant Dunfee was striding across the floor to Captain Valbuena.

She extended a hand, all brisk efficiency. "Richard? Good to see you, but any reason they sent you instead of minions?"

"Mia! Haven't seen you for ages." Captain Valbuena's smile showed far too much fang for comfort. "I think we should talk in your office."

The captain completely ignored Carrington as he brushed past, though he did give Wolf a nod. "Officer Wolf. I hope we can keep things civil this time."

"Yes, sir." He had to fight his instincts but managed not to growl—not for the ridiculous reasons a werewolf might have. Wolf just didn't appreciate him being rude to Carrington.

"Interesting," Vikash murmured, though he didn't elaborate.

With the care someone might take in walking around an agitated cobra, Carrington paced around the box. "Didn't he have rens with him?"

"He did." Vikash nodded to the parking lot. "They left."

"Insufferable elitist." Carrington did his offended sniff thing before marching back to his desk.

The vampire transport box, closed now, still sat on its gurney near the doors, where the officers from State had left it.

"I don't get it." Wolf stared at it, trying to see something other than a coffin. "Are they coming back?"

"Hmm." Vikash wandered over to his desk. "Probably not."

That didn't clear up anything. LJ drifted over to the box with Audacity riding in his inside pocket. He tapped on the lid with his sleeve, checking the seams and how it was attached to the gurney. Audacity scrambled out and plopped onto the floor to sniff the wheels.

"Baby girl, come away from there." Wolf crouched down and waited for Audacity to galumph over to him. "I don't think we should be messing with it."

Meerew.

"I know the rens touched it. Doesn't mean you should."

Mrrah?

"Rens are, um, they..." Wolf picked his cub up to scritch under her chin. "Vampire attendants, I guess. At State, every vamp has officers assigned, so it's more than just for transport."

Audacity wriggled to be let down and raced over to Carrington to pat his leg with one paw and mew at him.

"I don't have them because I don't need them, sweetie." Carrington bent down to speak to her. "I'm glad to have Amanda's help when necessary, but I'm a little more daylight mobile than the regular vamps."

She let out a kitten growl followed by a sneeze.

"I appreciate the support." He booped her tiny black nose with his forefinger. "But try to be polite while he's here, all right?"

With a squeak, Audacity ran around the desk and mewed at Amanda.

Amanda glanced down at the kitten, shaking her head. "Oh, no. Don't get me in the middle of this, little girl. You behave, like Carr says. Your *daddy* didn't even growl at him."

The door to the lieutenant's office clicked and their commander and her visitor chose that moment to come back into the squad room.

"Every cooperation, of course," Lieutenant Dunfee was saying. "Though I'm sure your loss will be keenly felt in Harrisburg, Richard."

"They'll muddle through without me for a bit, I'm sure." Captain Valbuena's eyes glittered as he surveyed the squad room — as if it were his new kingdom.

"I'll status Officers Wolf and Krisk as temporarily assigned to you," the lieutenant went on, her words a bit too clipped and professional. "They're already hip deep in this."

"Much appreciated." The captain stopped abruptly, head cocked. "Mia, I assume you know there's a kitten in your squad room?"

* * * *

Here they were at another Wednesday and poor Miriam wasn't getting her time alone with her son again. Jason couldn't feel too guilty since she'd been the one to invite him for dinner. *He's agitated*, Miriam had said on the phone. *I can't get him to settle and explain. Something about vampires.*

At least he could remember to bring over the ceramic birds he'd picked up the weekend before for Miriam. They'd discovered in conversations over dinners that they both had a yearning for dusty antique shops. Neither one of them was an expert in anything or even a rabid fan of any one sort of collectible or period. The appeal lay in poking around musty, stuffed-to-the-gills shops. Wolf didn't share their fascination but he indulged them both patiently, amused by their amusement.

When he let himself in, he was sure a wild animal had gotten in upstairs. Chuffs and growls accompanied the heavy pacing overhead.

"Miriam? Everything all right?" Jason called softly.

Miriam poked her head out of the study while Audacity skidded around the corner, mewing as she ran to him. "He said he didn't want to — couldn't — talk about it yet. I'm assuming something happened at work."

"Does this happen a lot?" Jason stared at the ceiling, mentally following Alex's footsteps as he crouched down to scoop up Audacity by feel.

"Not so much now that he's grown. The last time? I think he was in high school and some boys had been bragging about a dogfight. He'll settle when he's worked some of the frustration out." Miriam was frowning at the ceiling now, too. "But I do hate hearing him so upset."

Me, too. "Will I make things worse if I go up?"

"Oh, I can't imagine you would. Don't be offended if he's short with you, though."

"Understood." Jason put Audacity on the floor and braved the stairs. "Alex? I'm coming up."

The pacing didn't falter at this announcement, Alex's footsteps vibrating through the floorboards. It wasn't that Alex was stomping around like some clumsy human, oh, no. His footsteps were graceful, near silent — but a predator of his mass still made the floor tremble as he stalked from room to room.

Jason stopped out of the way at the top of the stairs. "Babe? Talk to me. You're worrying your pack."

Alex stalked by, waving an arm as he paced into the spare room. "Unprofessional. Unprofessional! He doesn't even— He'd only been there a couple of hours. How does that even? And Carr. And even Kash."

"Okay, I'm sure you're right. But who are we talking about?"

"That vampire captain!" Alex halted, chest heaving as he tried to bore holes in the wallpaper with his eyes.

Jason ventured a few steps closer. Only one vamp captain had ever come up in conversation. "You mean the one you almost had an Underworld fight with in Harrisburg?"

"Yeah. Him." Alex managed a sideways glance and a nod in acknowledgment, so he must've been coming back down from his caged tiger imitation. "He... State sent him. Carr called them about the woofen-poofs—"

"The what?"

"The metallic bird things. Kash says that's what they are."

One more step put him in arm's reach, so Jason put a hand on Alex's shoulder, stroking softly. "All right. Woofen-poofs. And State sent someone to, what? Claim them?"

"Someone to..." Alex squeezed his eyes shut and leaned in to Jason, who took it as a cue to wrap his arms around his wolf. "*Consult*. Yeah. That's the word they used."

"Did they say why? And they sent a *captain*?"

Alex turned into his embrace and hid his face against Jason's neck. "No. I guess... Maybe they think it's a thing? The hoax animals? And, um, yeah. Detective

Captain Valbuena. He's the head of the vamp detective squad up there."

"There has to be stuff they're not telling you."

"Yeah."

"But I don't think that's why you're upset."

The growl rumbled in Alex's chest again. "No. He pretended Carr was invisible. Told us having entities as consultants was unprofessional, especially since we didn't know where they came from." The growl grew louder, snarlier. "He called my Audacity a *pet*."

Part of Jason wanted to smile at this. More of him understood why it would tip his caring, gentle wolf into a state of barely controlled fury. "He didn't understand, Alex."

"Said there shouldn't be *pets* in the squad room."

Jason held him tighter as if he could hold Alex together. "He say anything about Edgar?"

"No." Alex's snort was more animal than human. "Edgar's a *familiar*."

"Well, okay. The captain's a jackass. But you can avoid him mostly, right?"

Alex deflated against him and Jason had to put one foot back to keep them upright. "No," he groaned. "Me and Krisk've been assigned to him."

"What… Assigned?" Now Jason was glad for Alex's bulk holding *him* up. Did that mean Alex was going to Harrisburg? Going *away*? Sure, it wasn't that far. Sort of. But too far to commute.

"Yeah. It's dumb. Vamps need assistants for going out in the field. In the daytime. They're called rens."

"You mean like Renfields? That's really condescending."

"I guess. Don't know how they feel about it. But he sent his rens back with the woofen-poofs. And we're stuck with him while he's here."

Oh, thank God. Not reassigned. That was a selfish thought. He knew it. "I'm sorry, babe. That doesn't sound fun. But I think you can still set some personal boundaries, even if he's a superior. Doesn't give him the right to be insulting."

Alex heaved a sigh so huge, it nearly lifted Jason off the floor. "Right. Professional. Adulting. I have to deal with this."

"You do. But you don't have to let him walk all over you, all right?" Alex nodded against his shoulder and some of the tension bled out of Jason. "Good. Get changed. I'll go keep your mom company and we'll all have a nice dinner."

"Oh. Yeah." Alex glanced down at his uniform as if surprised to see it still on his body before he wandered off to his room.

Audacity met him halfway down the stairs, mewing and endangering them both by running between his legs with every step. He finally scooped her up and plopped her onto her special chair at the kitchen table, the one with the extra cushions.

"Can I help with anything?" he asked Miriam.

"It's all under control. Just a pot roast I've had in the crockpot most of the day. You can set the table, though." Miriam didn't turn around from where she was lifting rolls off a cookie tray into a breadbasket. "Is he better?"

"He's calmer. I think he's still angry but he's processing better."

"Good. He would have calmed down eventually, but I'm glad you could accelerate the process."

Jason smiled, but Alex was a responsible person. He would've remembered he had people worried about him. *He didn't need me for that.*

When Alex jogged back down the stairs, he'd transformed into as-casual-as-possible Alex in sweats, stained T-shirt and bare feet. He scooped Audacity up and rubbed faces with her. "I'm sorry, kitten face. Didn't mean to scare you."

Audacity batted at her dad's nose with a series of scolding mews and he responded by gently catching her paw with a soft, fond growl. Once replaced in her seat, she sat prim and proper, the queen of all that her tiny self surveyed. Miriam served Audacity first, with a plate of roast and carrots cut into kitten-bite sized pieces. Jason still didn't approve of the eating at the table thing, but it wasn't his house and he'd verified that table food wasn't her primary diet.

When they'd sat down to pot roast heaven, since it was never 'just pot roast' or 'just anything' in Miriam's kitchen of perfect spices, Jason handed the box over to her. "These caught my eye last weekend. Thought you might enjoy them. They're supposed to be Japanese, but I can't be sure about that."

Miriam frowned but her eyes sparkled with anticipation as she opened the box. "Jason, you don't have to bring me things. But these are adorable." Her smile slipped through as she pulled out the little kingfisher and hummingbird ceramics.

Oddly, Alex went on alert, his hand trembling so hard he dropped his fork. "Mom? Can I see one of those?"

"Of course." She handed him the hummingbird. "Alex, what's wrong?"

He held the little statuette, turning it over in his hands. Finally, he turned it upside down and snuffled at the base. "This. This is the scent."

"What scent?"

"The one I couldn't place." Alex's gaze shot to Jason as he reached out to give the hummingbird back to Miriam. "At the jackalope sighting. In your backyard. The one that had Carr calling State because he thinks the sightings are *related*. It's… It doesn't make sense."

"Could you have smelled clay dust?" Miriam asked.

Alex pulled in a slow breath. "No. This is different. Once it gets heated, whatever they call it when they make pottery stuff, it smells different."

"Fired," Jason murmured absently.

"What?"

"When they heat clay for ceramics. Firing. Alex, you're not saying the animals are pottery, are you?"

"Not that. The animals smelled like…well, they smelled weird but they smelled like animals. The pottery scent was *near* where they were both times but not *them*." Alex sipped at his beer. "Sorry. Frustrating when you don't know where a scent comes from."

Dust bunny flashbacks. I get it, big guy. "You'll figure it out. But you don't have to do it this second, right?"

Alex nodded and plowed into his pot roast, a good indicator of his level of frustration, how fervently he channeled it into eating. Something they should talk about later, though Jason would feel like a hypocrite. He knew he ate for comfort, too.

"No one's taking your food, sweetie," Miriam said softly. It sounded like a reminder.

"Sorry." Alex reached for seconds and gave a few tiny pieces to his daughter when she demanded more. "I'm okay, Mom. It was a weird day."

"I'm sure." Miriam cleared her throat. "So, where is this Harrisburg vampire staying?"

"Captain's staying at the station." Alex shrugged. "Wheeled his travel box into the conference room for him."

Miriam's eyes went wide. "He's sleeping in your conference room? In a *box*?"

Alex concentrated on his plate, apparently unwilling to meet his mother's eyes. "I guess? I don't think he really sleeps... Much."

"So he's simply been abandoned there? Spending the night alone at the station?" Miriam's voice remained soft even as it edged toward horrified.

"Well, no." Alex shifted uncomfortably. "Carr and Amanda are on duty. Though, okay, they won't be there most of the time. LJ and Hunter are there. And Tim. And Edgar."

Miriam put her utensils down. "You've left him with a pair of known pranksters, a foul-mouthed raven, and... Granted, Tim's adorable, but he can't be much of a host. No wonder this vampire captain's so disagreeable if everyone treats him like this."

"Maybe that's not quite fair, Miriam." Jason stepped in where he probably shouldn't. "It doesn't sound like he gave them much notice."

"He was rude, Mom. He called Audacity a pet. He acted like Carrington wasn't even a person." Alex held up a hand when his mother opened her mouth to protest. "But I'll try to talk to him. He, um, might not listen. And might be fine staying in his box. I'll still ask. You're right. Doesn't mean we have to be rude just 'cause he's a...jerk."

"That's my Alex." Miriam half-stood to kiss his cheek. "Eat up. There's cake for dessert."

Jason winced. "I hope you didn't go to a lot of trouble."

"No trouble at all, dear. I was in Reading Terminal and it's always hard *not* to pick up a cake there."

After dinner, cake and cleaning up, Alex wallowed with Jason on the sofa watching *The Count of Monte Cristo*, both of them stuffed and sleepy. Half-reclined with his head nestled in the crook of Jason's shoulder, Alex dozed in and out, waking up intermittently to ask what had happened onscreen.

The whole evening had been so ridiculously comfortable, it almost drowned out the mice of doubt gnawing at the inner lining of Jason's brain.

Gnawed-on brain won over sense. "What's he like?"

"Who?" Alex asked around an adorable yawn.

"Detective Captain Vampire."

"Oh. Blond. Tall. Not buff big, but you can tell he's strong." Alex stopped to snuggle into a more comfortable position. "Handsome in a British kind of way. Are vamps ever plain looking? Must be something to that..."

"He's British?"

"I dunno. He might've been. Carr made it sound like he was turned a long time ago. I don't *think* he has an accent anymore. Didn't pay attention. He wasn't *nice* today but he's not an idiot. Guess he couldn't be. Detective captain and everything."

I hope he keeps being a jackass so you don't start to like him. Jason told the mice in his brain to settle down. They were making him stupid. Bad thing about brain mice — they didn't listen well at all.

Chapter Six

Wolf's determination to have a talk with Captain Valbuena temporarily derailed when he walked into a squad room in chaos. He arrived with Krisk just in time to feel the captain's bellow vibrate through the creaky floorboards.

"Get back here, you manufactured miscreants!"

LJ flew into the squad room with something held to his chest, Hunter right behind with an object clutched in her right sleeve. The bellowed words tattered around the edges and unraveled into an incoherent roar as Captain Valbuena tore around the corner after them. The perfectly pressed, smugly polished officer of the day before? Gone. His unbound hair was a wild mane around his head, his uniform shirt unbuttoned, his eyes tinged with the red of a vampire out of control.

Both coats floated high out of reach as LJ flipped a rude gesture at the captain and waved a *come on* at Edgar. Already intent on events, Edgar left his perch with a croaking chuckle. LJ tossed the object, the captain's hat, as Edgar flew overhead and he caught it neatly in his broad beak. Meanwhile, Hunter had zipped down to Tim and handed him her object, something small and black, which Tim had promptly popped inside and rolled his house as fast as he could under Kyle's desk.

Papers fluttered in an unnatural indoor breeze as the captain began to growl, the wind picking up as his growls grew louder. Several officers were startled into unintentional spurts of power. The coat rack beside Shira's desk shivered and danced before it crashed to the floor. An orange suddenly splatted against the far wall between the windows. Sparks erupted from Vance's fingertips and he had to rush to extinguish the paperwork on his desk.

In the shadows of the squad room's back corner, Carrington rose with deliberate care and stalked to the center of the room in the captain's line of sight. Without taking his eyes off Valbuena, he held out his hand and said in a conversational tone, "Edgar? Hat, please."

Edgar reversed course and arrowed toward Carrington, dropping the hat into his hand with bomber sight accuracy.

"Tim? Whatever you've squirreled away in there, if you please."

Tim's house peeked out from under Kyle's desk and somehow managed to look sheepish as it rolled across the floor to Carrington. An apologetic peep sounded from within the paper globe before Tim emerged with a black hair band.

Carrington placed it in the hat and held both out. "Captain? Yours, perhaps?"

"You *orchestrated* this with these *things* to humiliate me!" Valbuena bellowed, too far gone to be reasonable.

"I did no such thing, sir." Carrington stood his ground where someone else might have run to find a safe bolt-hole. "I hardly have time for nonsense like that."

"Vamp fight," Kyle whispered near Wolf's ear.

Maybe it was a stupid thing to do, but Wolf handed Audacity's carrier to Krisk and strode into the middle of the vampire standoff. He turned to Carrington first, hand outstretched. "Carr?"

The hesitation was just enough to indicate how on edge Carrington was but he finally drew in a deep breath and handed over the hat. Wolf turned and closed the distance between him and Valbuena, putting them nose to nose so that the captain's attention was all on him.

"Sir," Wolf said softly. "Maybe we should talk. Somewhere quieter."

Valbuena snatched the hat from Wolf's hands and stalked back down the hall toward the conference room. After a glance around the stunned-silent squad room, Wolf shrugged and followed. The captain hadn't said *not* to follow him.

By the time he caught up, Valbuena was yanking a brush through his hair so hard that Wolf winced. *What do I say here? Apologize? Explain?*

He cleared his throat, though the captain had to know he was there. "Are you okay, sir?"

"Abominations," Valbuena spat out. "This isn't a precinct of rejected candidates. It's full of freaks and unnatural creatures."

This coming from a vampire. "Sir, that might not—"

"And you!" Valbuena spun about to poke a finger at Wolf's chest. "What in all hells' names *are* you? You smell like werewolf and then you don't. Are you someone's science experiment?"

"No, sir." Wolf spoke slowly to keep the growl out of his voice. "I don't think that was called for."

Valbuena turned away and took the time to button his shirt and put his blond mane into a neat tail before he addressed Wolf again. "I apologize, Officer Wolf. This morning has been...fraught. And somewhat gnarly. I spoke out of turn."

"Understood, sir." Wolf picked a uniform jacket off the floor and shook it out. "I'm a wolf. I was cursed to live as a human. No, I can't change back into a wolf."

"Well, then." Valbuena shook his head as he gathered his scattered belongings into a case that fit neatly on a shelf under his transport box. "I'm doubly at fault for making assumptions. The accessible parts of your file are, shall we say, less than specific."

"It's all right, sir. Not something anybody'd think of."

"So, Officer Wolf who was a wolf, what did you want to speak to me about?"

Wolf had thought about this conversation, had rehearsed it several times, but now he couldn't remember any of it, of course. "Sir, we're sort of...all of us...like that. With the assumption stuff. We're...I know we're not usual. Not, um, normal...things. But we're not... We're not broken. Sir."

Valbuena stared at him, cool assessment that made Wolf want to squirm. "I see. And the entities? The ones who have most assuredly not been through the police academy?"

"They help because they've found a place here, sir." Somehow the words came easier when he wasn't talking about himself. "They've risked everything for us."

A hint of a smile ticked at Valbuena's mouth. "Perhaps I shouldn't have told them off for racing in the hallways?"

"Oh, we all do, sir. Just, um…nicely." Now that the captain had calmed down, Wolf felt more confident about speaking up. "And, sir?"

"Yes? What other grave crimes have I committed?"

"Audacity isn't a pet. She's my…my cub."

Captain Valbuena tilted his head, tapping his hat against his palm. "Ah. Well, then. Every day is bring your child to work day, is it?"

Wolf found he couldn't hold that clear, hyper-focused gaze any longer and stared at his shoes. "Lieutenant approves, sir. Audacity…she helps."

The captain's growl was more of a purr, vibrating through Wolf's bones. "Audacity. Aptly named. I will not tolerate disrespect and I will not have my orders disobeyed, Officer Wolf. Beyond that, I'll do my best not to incite any more riots."

"Yes, sir. Thank you." His mom's words from the night before finally caught up to him. "Oh, and sir? Do you need a place to stay? Should we, um, arrange a hotel or something?"

"No, no. This will do nicely for me. Transport back and forth from a hotel would be more trouble than it's worth. I *can* venture out in shaded or clouded daylight but I'd rather forego the discomfort." More hat tapping. "Stay close, Officer Wolf. You, I trust. You're steady. Sensible." Captain Valbuena patted Wolf's shoulder. "Do I look presentable?"

"Sir? Yes? There's a mirror —"

"Vampire." The captain sighed. "It's not that we don't have reflections. It's that we have trouble seeing them.

Something about the way our eyes process light makes reflections blurry."

Carrington doesn't have that prob – oh, right. "You look fine, sir. Very sharp."

"Thank you." There was the hint of a smile again, almost embarrassed. "I'm trusting you. Well, then. I suppose I should apologize."

Poised and perfect once more, Valbuena marched back out to the squad room with Wolf trailing anxiously. He expected hostility but the room was quiet, expectant. LJ and Hunter hovered near Carrington's desk. Tim sat bravely atop his house in the middle of the aisle with his police hat on. Most of the officers regarded the captain like a wary pack, though Krisk showed his unconcern by continuing to work through his emails on his computer. Carrington's face could have been carved from stone.

"Ladies, gentlemen, other beings." Valbuena nodded to LJ and Hunter. "I overreacted this morning. I'm out of my element and off schedule but that's no excuse. My apologies and my sincere hopes that we can move past this incident."

As apologies went, it wasn't a great one, but Wolf suspected it took all of the captain's willpower just to admit he was wrong. Kyle took a step forward. Shira stood up from her desk. Jeff swiveled his chair toward the captain. They all stopped, heads turning to Carrington.

Come on, Carr. You can do this. Be the bigger vamp. Wolf took note of the muscle tic in Carrington's jaw, ready to move if things went bad. He relaxed when Carrington raised one skeptical eyebrow instead of doubling down on the anger.

"Quite all right, sir," Carrington offered with precise, careful syllables, as if the words might cut him. "We understand our non-anthropoid colleagues can be a difficult adjustment."

Lieutenant Dunfee strode into the station on the last word, stopped in the act of pulling a file from her briefcase and glared around the room with narrowed eyes. "Everything all right here?"

"Yes, thank you." Captain Valbuena inclined his head toward her. "Small misunderstanding."

"Good. Since we're all here, I want everyone in the briefing room now."

Vance glanced up at the clock, "But, ma'am, it's not even—"

"Which part of *now* do you not understand, Virago? Because I don't think I can use smaller words."

The squad scrambled to lock computers and gather coffees as the lieutenant swept on through and down the hall. Valbuena shot Wolf a quirk of a smile before he followed. *He's not...flirting, is he? No, that would be stupid. He just wants an ally.* Since Lieutenant Dunfee had said *everyone*, Wolf scooped up Audacity on his way.

Mii-eew?

"I know it's not what we usually do. But I don't think it's fair to put you back in your carrier." He held her up to his face and got a nose bat in the process. "You have to stay still and quiet, though, okay? Listen to what the grown-ups are saying."

Mew.

She sat facing forward on his lap, straight and proper like a good junior officer, ears swiveling as Lieutenant Dunfee took the podium with Captain Valbuena standing at her left shoulder.

"Morning, everyone. Settle, please." She set her half-moon glasses on her nose and consulted her notes. Her words were bone dry as she continued, "I believe you've all met Detective Captain Valbuena. The captain will be with us for an unspecified period, investigating incidents that may be related to our unidentified rogue magic user. He will be given every cooperation and treated with the respect his rank deserves."

She peered over the top of her glasses at LJ, who managed a credible sleeve salute.

"Officers Wolf and Krisk have been seconded to Captain Valbuena for the duration of his visit, therefore, Dennis, Poole, see Officer Soren for adjusted schedules. The only other item I have this morning is regarding the upcoming wedding weekend after next. Official congratulations to two of our own, Officers Monroe and Soren. Health and happiness to you both."

"Thank you, ma'am," Kyle called out from his seat near the wall. "My mom keeps calling it *the day Vikash makes an honest man out of my son.*"

Kash put in softly, "To which his father responds, *it's far too late for that.*"

The lieutenant didn't quite roll her eyes. "All levity aside, we have official clearance to go remote for the day, so, yes, everyone who has been hounding me, you may attend. I assume I don't need to tell all of you to be vigilant and be prepared. Just in case."

The little spark of happy in Wolf's chest died at that. Yes, they understood. The last time they'd all managed to be in one place to celebrate, a monster had crashed the party. *Vigilant.* He could do that.

"I'll give the podium to Captain Valbuena now. Give him your full attention, if you please."

Valbuena flashed a smile as he stepped up and gripped the lectern with both hands. Even with a hint of fang, that bright smile transformed him from relatively handsome to devastating. *Though he might be using some vamp mind thing. Maybe.*

"Thank you, Lieutenant. Since there are, as was previously mentioned, *patterns* to the incidents in your city, I'd like to take a more proactive approach." Valbuena glanced down at the lectern, his expression serious again when he looked up. "I hesitate to say it, since we don't wish to borrow trouble, but incidents seem to have a way of finding the officers of the 77th. Between that and incidents involving citizens of wealth and power, I believe we have the perfect opportunity tomorrow."

"Setting us up, sir?" Greg asked and flinched when Shira kicked his ankle.

Thankfully, the captain was over his earlier rage and responded with a chuckle. "In a manner of speaking, yes. We have a rather unique opportunity tomorrow morning with the annual Shelter Friends charity run. I've arranged for this department to provide added security for the event and with all of you out there in plain sight alongside important personages? I believe the combined target may be irresistible."

Kyle raised his hand, though he didn't wait to be recognized. "Any idea who might be doing the targeting, sir?"

"My theory is that it's our rogue mage. The last monster didn't work, so this is the next escalation. Though how summoning hoax animals is being managed, I can't say. I will be in plainclothes, observing. I'd like Officer Soren to also—"

"Sir. I'm sorry. Remanded to desk duty."

"Oh, damn. Yes." Valbuena frowned, a bit of his earlier irritation returning as he shuffled through papers. He tapped something on the lectern as he pinned Carrington with his unnerving gaze. "Loveless... Helen Loveless. Relative?"

"Yes...sir." Carrington's voice was all civil chill. "That's my mother. She chairs the event every year."

"Splendid." The smile was back with a hint of feral. "Officer Loveless will be my additional plainclothes observer then. What better place than right where you belong, with your family?"

While Wolf sometimes struggled with subtext in conversation, even he knew that statement was half a dozen kinds of mean. Carrington was sitting far straighter than he usually did during roll call and briefing, the muscle tic back in his jaw. The threat of violence cracked and sparked in the air, but all he offered was a soft, "As you say, sir."

Amanda leaned over to whisper something in his ear. The corner of Carrington's mouth twitched and he stopped glaring quite so hard.

"Well, then." Captain Valbuena's eyes met Wolf's and the predatory smile softened. "We'll have more specifics for you later today."

There was an awkward pause as people shuffled in their seats, unsure if they'd been dismissed until Lieutenant Dunfee snapped, "Get to work, people! Out of my sight!"

Captain Valbuena caught Wolf's arm on the way out. He obviously had something to say but stopped to admire Audacity first. "She is absurdly cute."

Audacity reached a paw out to him. *Mew.*

"And it's lovely to meet you, miss." Valbuena's smile was so genuine and amused as he touched a finger to her pads and shook hands that Wolf was ready to forgive many of his prickly and snooty points.

"Sir? Did you need me?"

"Hmm. Need? Perhaps not yet." There it was again, the purr in his voice that might have been flirting. "I thought you might be able to answer a question. Do we have any contacts in Animal Control?"

* * * *

Jason had refrained from messaging Alex too much that day. Dealing with the vampire was going to monopolize most of Alex's social skills and he didn't want to interrupt at a bad time. Not to mention, he'd promised to meet Paul and Laura for lunch.

Of all of his siblings, his relationship with Paul was the most difficult. They'd been inseparable as kids — him, Lisa and Paul — since they were the three oldest and born one right after the other. A two year gap followed before the next oldest, Anna, had been born. But while he'd grown closer to Lisa over the years, the gulf between him and Paul had only widened.

This would be more of an ambush than a nice relaxed lunch. Even knowing that, Jason always held out some hope that this time would be different. The hope shrank when Paul's message said to meet him for a twelve-thirty reservation. They couldn't just go to a nice sandwich shop or the dim sum place near the hospital where Paul worked, of course. It had to be somewhere chic that took lunch reservations.

Money? Sure, Paul and Laura made obscene amounts between the two of them, but it was more the conscious need to make sure everyone knew that made Jason crazy, never able to simply relax and enjoy something without looking at the prestige and the price.

Jason arrived a few minutes late to Paul glaring at his watch.

"Sorry. Couldn't find a parking spot. No Laura?" Jason's heart sank a little farther. Laura's conversation was often limited, she tended to live inside her own head, but her presence did keep Paul from bringing up certain subjects.

"She's still in the OR. Complications on a heart valve replacement." One last scowl at the sun before he opened the door to the restaurant. "I don't have much time either."

"I'm sure your patients are willing to wait a few minutes if you're running late."

Paul shook his head as the host led them to a table by the window. "I hate being one of those doctors. A one-thirty appointment should be at one-thirty, not two."

Always wound too tight, his younger brother, but at least he was conscientious. They both ordered fussy salads, Paul because he liked them and Jason because he wasn't going to sit through a heart health lecture for ordering beef. They talked about Paul's kids for a bit and his joint practice with Laura – his cardiology to her cardiac surgery – and there the small talk ran dry.

Paul took five uncomfortable seconds to pounce. "You have to stop all this, you know. You're really making Mom and Dad miserable."

"Stop all what?" Jason pushed walnuts around his plate, his hackles already rising. He knew exactly what Paul meant, but why make it easy?

"This being gay thing. Bad enough that you'd remind them of it sometimes. Now you have to shove it in their faces with a…a boyfriend? A *white* boyfriend. Christ, Jason. I just can't."

Jason shrugged. "No one's ever asked you to hide who you are."

"Of course not. I'm not — " Paul broke off with a wave of his hand. He didn't need to say *abnormal* to make his point. "You need to finally grow up. Get a real job. Find a nice girl to start a family with."

"That's the point, isn't it? Girl and love won't happen, no matter how many times you say it."

Paul managed to take a bite and roll his eyes at the same time. "You don't have to be in *love*. Just someone you like. Gay men do it all the time. Make Mom and Dad happy and stop leading this half-life."

"I have a whole life, thanks." Jason put his fork down. "Alex — "

"Yes. Alex. That's what has Mom worried. She ignored your sleeping around when nothing was ever serious. Now? You've brought home this cop, *gege*, who keeps clothes at your house. We're not blind. We can all see how serious it's getting."

"I know I wasn't subtle. Maybe it was too much, too soon for Mom." Jason stared out the window, wondering where this was going. "I'm sorry about that."

"*Jason*, you're not listening. Not that you ever did." Paul huffed. "We all see it coming. This special unit cop with superpowers. He's not staying around long. Not when there have to be other cops like him. Not when you have nothing to offer him. If you let this go too far, he'll break your heart. Break it off now, before you're in too deep. Before he leaves you."

"I don't think this is any of your — "

"Family who worries about you or lover who's going to leave you soon. Your choice."

Moving with exaggerated care, afraid if he made any sudden move it would turn into smacking his brother, Jason put his napkin on the table and left a few bills for his lunch. "I'm going to pretend you didn't say that. I'll talk to you soon."

He tried his best to walk out at a normal pace but once he reached the pavement, his steps became an angry stalk. It was one thing for his family to constantly put him down, which they did in little digs and jabs about not going to grad school and not having a *real* job and not starting a family. The endless comparisons to his successful younger siblings, the reminders that he was the eldest and should have been the example—sure, all that got old. But it was directed at him alone. Now, they were dragging Alex into the family drama.

Jason had expected it. No way to avoid it if he was trying to have his family accept them as a couple. But the consensus reaction nagged at him. He hadn't expected his family to become a Greek chorus saying he wasn't good enough for Alex.

Maybe that meant it was painfully obvious to everyone but him. He wasn't good enough for Alex, and soon Alex would figure that out. The whole *family or Alex* choice was stupid. He wasn't about to make that choice.

But the niggling doubts that kept gnawing at his brain told him that soon he wouldn't have to. Alex would be gone.

* * * *

It was a pretty day for the Shelter Friends charity run, at least. Jason didn't have a problem standing with the volunteers from the shelters and he knew Julie didn't either. They'd known most of these folks for years and saying hello to the dogs they'd brought with them wasn't a chore at all.

Still, he wasn't sure he understood why Animal Control had been asked to send officers. Alex had mentioned something along the lines of, *you have better equipment than we do in case something shows up*, which wasn't ominous at all, not one bit. There he was, though—straight and tall under one of two canopies flanking the stage. Just the sight of his Alex made any niggles of worry worth it.

With a bichon frise who didn't want to be put down tucked under his arm, Jason made his way over to say hello. Odd, Krisk wasn't anywhere in sight, or maybe not so odd since he might have distressed the attending dignitaries. The person standing at Alex's shoulder had to be the vamp detective. Had to be. He was as pale as Carrington, dressed in a light gray suit and hat with broad mirror sunglasses obscuring half his face. A frown furrowed that face and his shoulders hunched. This was not a happy vampire.

"Hey, Officer Wolf." Jason gave Alex's shoulder a squeeze as he eased in beside him. "Anything we can help with this morning?"

"Jason." Alex spared a quick smile for him. "Captain, this is Jason Shen, from AC. Jason, this is Detective Captain Valbuena, from Harrisburg."

A little twitch went with the introduction. Jason couldn't tell if it was tension from being around the vampire or if Alex was struggling to remain professional and not say *my boyfriend*.

Or not say it for some other reason. Shut up, brain mice. Just shut up.

Tremors ran through the captain's hand as he extended it for a desultory handshake. "Thank you for joining us, ACO Shen. As I understand it, you've been present for other atypical beast sightings."

"I was. Not sure how much help we'd be since we don't know what we might run into. But we'll do our best." The bichon in Jason's arms had bared its teeth at the captain. It snapped as he pulled his hand away.

"I'm afraid dogs don't find me pleasant company." Captain Valbuena's smile was charming but something else lurked underneath. Something that made Jason's scalp prickle.

"Jason, maybe, um…" Alex made a motion that could only be meant as surreptitious shooing. "Maybe go say hi to Carr?"

"I'll do that." Jason shot him a look that he hoped conveyed *oh, we're talking later.* "Captain, I don't mean to sound rude but are you sure you're okay out here?"

"I'm perfectly fine, thank you," Valbuena snarled, his charm replaced by a hint of fang.

"Great to hear, sir. Nice to meet you." Jason tucked the bichon closer and made his way through the crowd to the other tent where Carrington waited, also in light-colored clothes, hat and shades, though *his* hat looked well-loved.

"Jason." He raised a glass of ice in salute.

"Hey." The dog in Jason's arms didn't growl at Carr. This didn't exactly surprise him. "Can I ask you a couple of questions about the vamp from State?"

Carrington snorted. "Not if you want an unbiased opinion."

"Is he really that bad?"

"Yes." Carrington scowled at his glass. "No. I'm not being fair. He wasn't the worst of them and certainly wasn't one of my regular tormentors. Still. He swallowed the *vampire abomination* propaganda about me just as quickly as the others. His *sire—*"

"Hey. I'm sorry. Didn't mean to bring up painful history. Carr, don't break the glass." Jason waited until Carrington's hand relaxed its death grip. "Just general questions like should he even be out here?"

"No. No, he really shouldn't. Stubborn egotist. His thinking mostly likely runs along the lines of *if that weakling Loveless can do it, so can I.* Idiot." Carrington stole a quick glance over that way. "Again, biased opinion. In a more unbiased assessment, he doesn't look like he's managing well at all. That's why we assigned Krisk and Wolf to him while he's visiting. In case he needs physical rescue. He'll manage for a bit in the shade, but even that's going to wear him down quickly. I give him half an hour at the very most before he faints."

"Has he..." Jason didn't know how to phrase the question without sounding like he was in high school. "How is he with Alex?"

Carrington stared at him, though hard to tell what his eyes were saying behind the mirror shades. "Valbuena seems to have taken quite a liking to him. A little odd, since I would've thought the werewolf issue would carry over. Apparently not. But then, our Wolf isn't a victim of hormonal poisoning like most of the werewolves I've met."

A liking. What does that even mean? I don't like *how close he's standing to Alex. And I have to stop thinking like this. Now.*

"Carrington? Who do you have there?"

A woman in an expensive summer-weight suit clipped up to them in sensible heels, entourage in tow. The echoes of Carrington in her face were unmistakable. His mother.

Carrington allowed her to tuck her hand into the crook of his elbow. If he rolled his eyes, once again, the sunglasses offered perfect cover. "Mom, this is Jason Shen, the city's finest animal control officer. Jason, this is my mother, Helen Loveless." He indicated the rest of the party in turn with languid waves of his hand. "My father, Carrington Sr. His colleague, Drake Entwhistle. Dr. Cora Hibbert, from biology at Penn. And Dr. Garrett Hayes, to whom the 77th is forever grateful."

"Now, now, Carrington. It was only money," Dr. Hayes objected with a soft laugh. Average in every way, Dr. Hayes didn't look like a mover-and-shaker, but the company he kept said otherwise. Though on second appraisal, his suit wasn't off-the-rack and those shoes had to cost as much as Jason's truck.

Carr leaned his head closer to Jason. "Dr. Hayes provided when the state wouldn't. May have only been money, but it helped repair and equip the station house the city gave us."

"We all very much admire Garrett's generosity," Mrs. Loveless said in a tone that said she was tired of hearing about it. "But who do you have there, Officer Shen?"

"This little guy?" Jason turned the dog so the event's benefactors could see him. "This is Hector. He's a bichon frise, a newer arrival at one of the shelters. Found in an apartment laundry room."

"Isn't he just the sweetest thing?"

While Hector hadn't reacted at all to Carrington, he snapped at Helen's reaching hand, which she snatched back with a surprised *Oh!*

"Probably the crowd, ma'am." Jason managed to keep a straight face, though his stomach hurt from holding in laughter. "The pups get a little sensory overloaded. Best to be cautious."

"Yes. Thank you."

Apparently, that had been a dismissal since the posh crowd swept on past him and up the steps to the stage. Carrington stayed behind in the shade.

"You're most welcome to stay with me if you like. We're seeded through the crowd." Carrington pointed with his chin to several familiar officers. "Keeping watch. Perhaps nothing will happen, but I have to concede the point to Valbuena. This combination of money, outside venue and us seems irresistible if the hoax animals are being sent by our stalker mage."

"I don't think I want to know why your department has a stalker mage."

"We may have. Perhaps. It may simply be our paranoia and State's paranoia combining to see connections where there aren't any. Still. The city requires a police presence for events, so why not use us? It hurts absolutely nothing. Except perhaps certain vampire detective captains."

They both leaned out past the stage to check on the other canopy. Alex or some other sympathetic soul had snagged a chair for the captain.

"Aberrant vampire, one. Normal vampire, zero," Carrington murmured.

Jason tried his best to ignore the fact that the aforementioned normal vamp was practically clinging as Alex helped him take a seat. "So where's Manda? And Krisk?"

"Krisk is back at the station with Kash. Monitoring. Just in case. Manda has Eva today." Carrington saluted toward his partner across the parkway. "And Kyle has Jeremy. They've proved steady so far. Eager to learn. Not easily shaken. Well, Eva more than Jeremy in that regard."

"Good to hear." Jason hefted his canine passenger. "Well, I better get Hector back to his shelter peeps since he's here as a potential adoptee."

"Best of luck, Hector." Carrington nodded to the dog. "Oh, will we see you at the wedding?"

"Of course. Can't make Alex go alone." Jason tossed back over his shoulder. "Might even wear a tie."

"That alone would be worth the price of admission," Carrington called after him.

Yes, he'd go to the wedding because Kyle and Kash were good people and a great couple and he was trying to get over his judgmental self about weddings as heteronormative distractions from real issues. They *wanted* the outward commitment and legal terms of marriage and they had that right. Jason just hoped Alex would still want him to tag along by then.

* * * *

Wolf didn't have a lot of experience with regular vampires but he could tell this had been a dumb idea. The captain was *wilting*. There wasn't any other word for it and he wasn't even out in the sun. Carrington had tried to advise him — what to watch for, what to do — but he'd also said there was no saving a man from his own ego.

"Thank you." Captain Valbuena still clutched his arm after he'd managed to sit. "Just a little dizzy. Much better."

"I hope so, sir. Just lemme know if we need to get you out of here and I'll back the van right up to your chair."

He got a frown for that so he figured he'd have to wait until the captain had passed out. Meanwhile, Carrington lounged against a pole under the other canopy looking pleased with himself. Who knew that vampires played daylight chicken?

Wolf's head jerked up as he caught a now-familiar scent. Pottery dust. "Sir? There's—"

A strange *pop* cut off his words, followed by a hard projectile pinging off the tent pole closest to Wolf's ear.

"Get down!" Wolf roared as he vaulted onto the stage to put himself between Mrs. Loveless and the shooter. He engulfed her small frame with his, yanking her down to the stage decking. "Down! Shots fired!"

Carr hurtled in from the right to take down Dr. Hayes, who stood staring in the direction of the shots, most likely in shock. Carr began barking orders as he searched the crowd for the shooter. "Everyone stay low. Make your way off the stage but stay *down*. Wolf, can you see where it's coming from?"

Another projectile pinged off the podium and bounced onto the stage. Wolf followed the angle of the shot to a tree on the other side of Eakins Oval. "Over there, Carr. To the right."

"I have it." Carrington crouched, about to leap off the stage. "What in the name of all…"

Wolf followed his gaze to the missile lying on the stage. It wasn't a bullet. It was…a dirt pellet? What sort of weapon fired hard-packed dirt?

"Make sure everyone gets away from the stage." A low growl rumbled from Carrington. "I'm going after this cretin."

The officers in the crowd were already clearing the open space in front of the stage, getting civilians out of the line of fire. Jason had hustled the shelter workers with their furry charges behind the animal control truck. Carrington hurled himself off the stage, blurring as he raced toward the tree while Amanda followed, hand on the grip of her still-holstered weapon. Wolf lost sight of both of them for an instant as the crowd bunched and dispersed. When he spotted Carrington again, the vampire was at the base of the tree. He leaped into the branches where there was a horrific screech and scuffle, leaves shaking and falling.

The thing that fell out of the tree with Carrington wrapped around it? Definitely not a human shooter. It had…three legs? No. Two short legs and a long tail. As Carrington appeared to get the best of it, though, the legs *extended*, lifting him from the ground as the strange creature bucked and kicked. Jason ran toward them now with one of those hinged net frames he called a nabber.

About to go help, Wolf yelped and ducked as another dirt pellet grazed his shoulder. The shot had come from the other side of the circle. *Of course.* All the other weird animals had come in pairs. This one had a partner, too. He vaulted off the stage and headed in that direction, trying to pinpoint the second creature's location. A rush of air and a blur of grey blew past him.

Oh, no. "Sir! That's not a good idea!" *Yeah. Like a certain hardheaded vampire officer's gonna listen.*

Wolf hurried after him, dodging around civilians. Valbuena was faster than Carr, scary fast, and reached the tree before Wolf had picked out the right one. A branch knocked the captain's hat off as he leaped for the creature, then the scene from across the circle repeated. Rustling, shrieking, the fall from the tree and the thud that followed.

Except it was only Captain Valbuena who fell from the tree and lay in a heap in the grass. Wolf lifted a large man out of his way instead of doing the dodge-dance with him and sprinted the rest of the way. Kyle and Jeremy caught up to them from the other direction as the creature in the tree began firing pellets down at the captain. He curled into a ball, arms over his head — probably the smartest thing he'd done all day.

"Like we practiced, okay?" Kyle was saying to Jeremy.

Jeremy nodded, shaking out the net Kyle handed him. While Wolf dove for the stricken vampire, covering him with his own body, Jeremy took Kyle's hand and closed his eyes. Wolf peeked out from under his arm to watch, dirt projectiles hitting his back and shoulders every few seconds like rocks from a slingshot. Jeremy rose slowly from the ground and Kyle gained altitude with him, nearly in sync.

"That's it, Jer. Steady. While Wolf has it distracted."

"Thanks," Wolf muttered, though he turned his head to snarl at the thing in the tree to make sure it concentrated on him.

One of the strangest things he'd ever seen, it had an ovoid head with an elongated snout it could round into its shooter. A chicken-sized body sat atop those bizarre legs that looked like telescoping pipes with a long, kangaroo-like tail helping it balance on the branch. The animal's brown covering reminded Wolf of a kiwi, somewhere between hair and feathers. The vindictive thing fired at his eye and he barely ducked in time.

Jeremy levitated even with it and it turned too late to prevent him from throwing the net over its head. There was a surreal struggle as Jeremy lost concentration and tipped sideways, but he got the net tightened around the animal before he smacked into the tree, Kyle got his freehand on the net and they all fell hard.

"Not quite how I envisioned it, but you did it." Kyle grinned as he helped Jeremy up. "How's Captain Valbuena?"

"Not sure yet." Wolf sat back to assess. "I'm thinking not so good."

Not so good turned out to be bad. The vampire's hands were blistered from the sun. His eyes were too swollen to open. The only response Wolf got from calling to him was a weak, ineffective growl.

"Jeremy, take the...whatever that is to the animal control truck. Ask if they'll bring both to the station." Wolf pushed back his hat and ruffled at his sweaty hair. "Kyle, can you get me a blanket, sheet, something to cover the captain, please?"

"Back in a second." Kyle handed the discarded hat to Wolf and ran off to where the squad cars sat.

If it had been winter, Wolf would've at least had a jacket to cover the exposed skin. As it was, he situated the hat so it shaded Valbuena's face and tucked his poor burned hands underneath him. He knew vamps and sun didn't mix. Everyone knew that. He just hadn't known how bad it could be with a regular vamp.

A rustling in nearby shrubs startled Wolf and he turned, snarling, hoping there wasn't a third shooter thing lurking. The leaves parted and a head poked out at the same moment the pottery dust scent hit Wolf's nose like a rake handle to the face. It *was* a third one but tiny, no bigger than his hand, and though it moved, he had the strange certainty that he wasn't watching a creature of flesh and blood. Its lines were too smooth, its smell too distinct. This miniature version was ceramic.

Before he could reach out and snag it, the ceramic creature fled, making Wolf wonder if he'd been out in the sun too long as well.

"Hey. Best I could do." Kyle returned with a regulation blanket from his cruiser.

"Did you see that?"

"See what?"

"A pottery animal." Wolf shook his head. "I'll tell you about it later. Think I need to talk to Carr about this when we get back."

Kyle stared at him for a long moment. "You know, these are the moments I really miss simple old armed robberies."

Chapter Seven

"But he'll be okay, won't he?" Jason juggled phone and keys as he opened his front door.

"I...probably? Lieutenant's with him now." Alex's voice was strained — tired, uncomfortable, hard to tell. "I don't feel right leaving yet."

"Hey, it's okay. I get that." Jason eased through the frantic dance of canine greeting and snuffling. "I'm here if you change your mind later, but I'm kinda beat, too. Don't worry so much."

Alex heaved an unsteady breath. Little meows came from nearby. "No, Jason's not mad at us. We'll go see his pack another day. Sorry, Audacity knows when I'm talking to you."

"Aww, tell her we'll all miss her." Jason managed a smile. "You go do what you need to, babe. Just don't try to be responsible for everything."

They hung up but things still felt off. Good bet that it was mostly Jason feeling off, or all him. The dirt-slinging critters had been weird enough. They hadn't just been frightened or aggressive. They'd been *hostile*. He'd never seen anything like it and he'd never been so relieved to hand an animal over to another agency. Kash had taken one look at them and said they were tripoderos. Apparently, he was making it part of his job to know *all* the hoax animals.

He hadn't been able to see Alex when he'd visited the station, since he was back with the captain. Restraining him, which didn't sound good at all.

Jason shook his head at himself as he put down the dogs' food dishes, then started the can opener to call the cats. *Reading into things. Ever since the woofen-poofs.* Tybalt stood on his hind legs and put his giant kitty paws on Jason's hip, patting and reminding in his surprisingly small meows.

Babies first. All of them. He left all the furred peeps chowing down, hurried out to feed the rabbits, then went to check on Chien Long the iguana. He'd eaten all his greens like a good miniature dragon and still had some of his colorful iguana food in the shapes of tiny fake fruit. This room at the side was always the quietest place in the house, so Jason sat in the creaky desk chair beside Chien Long's terrarium to try to unwind.

Should get something to eat. At least get some water.

His brain kept replaying the vampires, both of them, risking themselves to go after the critters even though they assumed someone was shooting. Captain Valbuena dashing out into the blazing sunshine. *Serve and protect.* Like Alex, they had heroes' hearts.

Like Alex, who had put himself between flying projectiles and civilians. Who had rushed to save the captain when he was in trouble. Who had wrapped that fallen captain up as best he could and gently carried him to the waiting transport van. Alex, who had insisted on riding with the captain because he was worried. Alex...whose duty compelled him to stay after hours even though there probably wasn't much he could do.

Alex, who, as a wolf, had protecting those under his care encoded in his very DNA. A hero born.

"While I'm the local dog catcher."

Chien Long snorted at him, which had more to do with clearing calcium crystals from his nose than commentary, but it was good timing.

"I know. I'm being stupid. Just wonder why he's with me some days, right?"

The conversation clearly no longer interested Chien Long, who climbed up on his branch and closed his eyes.

* * * *

"He needs to eat." Lieutenant Dunfee leaned against a desk, tired enough to unbend that far. "I've done what I can, but he will become both weaker and more feral if he doesn't feed."

Wolf looked between the lieutenant and Carrington. "Can he have some of yours?"

"No. Mine doesn't have all the necessary components." Carrington puffed his cheeks as he blew out a hard breath. "And regular vamps require it directly from the source. It's not that they're picky or demanding. It simply doesn't work otherwise."

"Damn him for sending all his rens back." A muscle in Lieutenant Dunfee's jaw ticked. "Unlikely we could get one here for him before midnight, if they're even on call."

Carrington gave her a cautious sideways glance. "And that wouldn't look good for us, would it? Already under a black cloud and then we're unable to take care of the officer they sent us."

"I hope you're not hinting that I *buy* him a meal, Loveless."

"Gods forbid, ma'am. How would you ever put in a reimbursement requisition for that?"

The lieutenant didn't laugh — in fact, her frown deepened. "And you better not be suggesting that I feed him."

Carrington held up both hands to fend off that glower. "Never. Your magic and vamp might not mix. Though I certainly can't. Vamp to vamp is little better than poison."

They turned toward Amanda and Eva in the far corner, who both looked up from their paperwork with identical scowls and a simultaneous, "No."

Wolf stood. The only other person in the squad room was Krisk and *that* wouldn't work. "I'll do it."

Five heads whipped toward him.

"It makes sense. I've got all human parts. No magic." Wolf shrugged. "And I'm big enough to hold him down if he's, um... If he..."

"If the captain is somewhat reasoning deficient," Carrington supplied in a dry tone.

"Yeah."

Lieutenant Dunfee pinned him with a hard look. "Be sure, Officer Wolf. He's not himself and may not be gentle." She sighed and ran a hand over her face, more depleted than Wolf had ever seen her. "I appreciate you volunteering, but I hope it's not out of obligation or guilt."

"No, ma'am. I'm just the only choice that makes sense."

"You want Loveless with you?"

Wolf shook his head. "I'll leave the door open. Yell if I need help."

A tug on his arm stopped him and he found himself kitten-assaulted with Audacity climbing his shirt and mewing as if her volume control had broken. She climbed all the way to his collar, crying frantically in his face.

"I'm just going to the conference room, little girl. Not leaving you. Krisk's right there if you need a lap."

Carrington cocked his head to study her. "I think she has larger concerns."

"She—" It hit him city-bus-running-a-red-light hard. "Oh. *Oh*. Sweetie, I'm not going to let the captain *eat* me. He just needs to drink a little. Like…a mosquito. But bigger."

A choking, sputtering sound erupted from Carrington. He turned it into a polite cough. "I'm sure the captain would appreciate the apt comparison."

Miw?

Wolf ignored his still snickering colleague. "Really. I have to help and it won't hurt me. Be back before you know it."

Mee-ew.

That sounded a little too much like *you'd better be*.

"Promise." One claw at a time, Wolf extracted his kitten from the front of his shirt and handed her off to Carrington.

"Lovely. Cat hair all over my uniform again." Their vampire sighed, though he cuddled Audacity close.

When Wolf reached the conference room, the door was closed. This only happened when Lieutenant

Dunfee had too many visiting dignitaries to fit in her office. *For privacy since he's in bad shape? To keep Captain Valbuena in?* Not a happy thought. He eased the door open, leaving it ajar as promised.

The traveling box sat with its lid up, but it was empty. The captain wasn't sprawled in any of the chairs. *Crap. He's in here, though. I hear him.*

Wolf had time for that quick thought before something slammed into his left side and he found himself in a tangle of limbs, fingers digging into his arms with bruising force and sharp teeth snapping at him.

"Sir! It's Wolf!" He tried to find any hint of sense in the captain's swollen red eyes as he held off those fangs. "You don't want to do this."

Easy enough to toss the captain across the room, but injuring him further was the exact opposite of what Wolf had come in for. A hard shove and a roll got him up. A quick pounce got him behind his feeding-crazed assailant so he could pin the captain's arms to his sides.

"Captain! Richard!" Wolf shouted in his ear, hoping the shock of a loud noise so close would break through. "I'm here to help you. To feed you. But you have to calm down."

Snarling and hissing, Valbuena continued to struggle. Not that holding him still was a challenge, but how in the world was Wolf supposed to get him to feed instead of trying to rip his throat out? *Turn on the lights and stun him? Maybe.* It had worked for Commander Rahway, but the conference room lights wouldn't be as shocking as a work light to the face.

Without loosening his bear hug, he reached up and pinched the captain's nose closed. Hard.

"Ow!" The snarling turned into weak sputtering. "Whad id all hells?"

"Sir, it's Wolf. Lieutenant Dunfee said you need blood. I'm here to feed you, but I'm not gonna let you do it when you're crazy." Wolf eased his hold on Valbuena's nose but nothing else. "Can you try being *not* crazy for a minute?"

"That was a terrible sentence, Officer Wolf. You should be ashamed," Valbuena whispered. "Everything hurts. I...keep blacking out."

You keep vamping out, you mean. "I've got you, sir. If I give you a wrist, is that enough?"

Valbuena shook his head carefully. "Too slow. Might try to...won't be good."

"Damn. Okay. But if you start going feral, you won't get much of a feeding." Wolf got his back against the wall and pulled the captain up more comfortably against him, settling him so he could reach Wolf's throat. "That work?"

"I don't usually... Not without... I *do* apologize beforehand, Wolf."

"Captain, I'm thinking you only have so much time before you go out again. Better get going with your breakfast."

Valbuena snuffled at his throat and Wolf got that. Smelling food before you ate it made sense. Then he licked a soft line up Wolf's jugular, which did all sorts of work-inappropriate things to his insides. *Gah.* This was all sorts of wrong.

"Well, then," Valbuena whispered against his throat.

A moment later, he pierced skin with a sound that reminded Wolf uncomfortably of someone biting into a sausage casing. He left leg twitched and thumped at the strange mix of pain and erotic rush. The teeth were needle sharp, so it wasn't any worse than getting an IV, but the lips sucking at his throat, the strange pull of the feeding that tugged all the way to his balls, the way Captain Valbuena clutched at his shirt with both hands—all more intimate than Wolf had been expecting.

No wonder rens got attached and no wonder vampires' lovers got addicted. *Concentrate, dummy, or you'll end up passed out on the floor.* The feeding was frantic at first, desperate whimpers coming from the captain as he sucked hard. Wolf had a bad moment when he was sure he would have to get rough so he wouldn't become an empty vampire Slurpee. Slowly, Valbuena settled, his hands relaxing, his body slumping in Wolf's arms as the hard pulls gentled and slowed.

It didn't take much before vampire metabolism took over and visible healing started. The captain's poor swollen hands shrank to a normal size, the skin no longer stretched tight. The angry red returned to vampire pale.

With a soft sigh, Valbuena stopped on his own, licking at Wolf's throat again to close the bites. "Thank you," he whispered, though he didn't seem in any hurry to move.

"All right there, sir?"

"Much better. I'll need to supplement tomorrow night—" He broke off when Wolf let out a hard breath. "I won't trouble you for it. Not at all safe."

"Okay. Sir, um..." *How do I say get off me politely? Please let me the hell up?* "Can I, um, help you up?"

"If you would be so kind. Not sure how steady I am."

Wolf got his arms around Valbuena again and simply lifted him to his feet as he stood.

"Such strength." Valbuena's smile was hesitant, maybe embarrassed. "And it never fades."

"I wouldn't say never, sir. Just not in the sunlight. I don't do too great if I haven't eaten all day, though."

Valbuena chuckled and patted his chest, still leaning against him. "You must think me terribly full of myself. Did I make too much of a hash of things today?"

"You did fine, sir. Helped catch one of the tripoderos." Maybe that was stretching the point, but it felt unkind to say otherwise.

"Ah, so we have a name for them."

Wolf turned with him, since the captain seemed determined to go out to the squad room. "Yes, sir. And some other developments. Don't know how much help they'll be."

"Excellent. Good man." A little of his natural poise was returning with his correct coloring, though the smile remained unsure. Valbuena took his arm as they headed into the corridor. "I can't thank you enough. You need to let me take you out to dinner. Buy you a drink, at least."

"Sir, um." *Not ethical, not advisable, not somewhere we should be going.* "Maybe buy the squad a pizza? That would be nice. I love pizza."

Captain Valbuena's smile froze. Then he nodded. "Of course. My white knight is impeccably moral. My apologies, Sir Galahad."

Weird. If Carrington had said that, it would've come out snarky and sharp. Captain Valbuena wasn't at all sarcastic, though. He sounded regretful, disappointed. Wolf nearly apologized but the charming smile returned.

"Well, then. Let's go speak to your lieutenant. Let her see I haven't damaged one of her officers while you tell me about these new developments."

* * * *

Jason stirred at the sound of the door closing downstairs and stared bleary-eyed at the clock. It had to be Alex since no one was sounding an alarm. Eleven-thirty wasn't that late, really. A little weird, maybe. He had been expecting Alex to go home after such a long day.

The man himself appeared in the doorway two minutes later with Audacity tucked in the crook of his arm. "Hey. Was hoping I wouldn't wake you."

"How were you and the cub going to crawl into bed with me without waking me up?" Jason chuckled as he sat up and stuffed a pillow behind his head.

Alex's forehead wrinkled. "I would've gone down to sleep on the couch if you were sleeping."

"Sort of defeats the purpose of coming over to sleep with me. Come on. Get undressed and get in here. You look like you're done."

Audacity batted to be put down and Alex set her on the bed with Jason while he peeled out of his dirt and grass-stained uniform. The more he peeled, the more concerned Jason grew. Round bruises dotted Alex's back and arms. Suspiciously finger-shaped sets decorated his biceps. There were even two small ones on his throat.

"Babe? What the hell happened? You're...Christ."

When Alex had dropped his pants, there were even bruises on his ass. He turned his head to follow Jason's gaze. "Oh. Tripodero pellets, mostly. Those things shoot hard."

"Mostly?" Jason slid out of bed and touched one of the bruises on Alex's upper arm. "Tripoderos don't have fingers."

Alex busied himself with getting his feet untangled from his pants and briefs. "I, um... Captain Valbuena was...he shouldn't have been out in the sun."

"Okay." Jason backed off. Crowding Alex wouldn't help him spit out whatever had happened. "I can't argue that."

"He got kinda...it was bad. Lieutenant said he was going feral. He needed to feed."

"But from *you*?"

Alex turned his back to drape his clothes on the back of the chair. A hint of growl colored his voice when he finally said, "No one else there could deal with him."

I don't even...did they have sex? They must have. Vampires can't feed without sex, right? Except Carrington. But all the others? Maybe? I don't care. I shouldn't. Exclusive was never a huge thing for me before. Except that we have been. I haven't...not since Alex. I haven't wanted to since Alex. But, oh god. A vampire. A handsome, brave, protect and serve vampire – stop it.

"Are you okay?" Jason cleared the embarrassing squeak from his voice. "I mean...is it like a donation at the blood bank?" *I can't believe I just said that.*

Alex shot him a puzzled look. "Maybe? I don't know what that's like. The doctors told me I should never donate. Just in case."

Until now. "Yeah. Okay. I haven't been able to for a long time since I never go a full twelve months without having sex." *Babbling and he's got that Perplexed Alex look.*

"Did you eat something after? Are you dizzy? Tired?"
Of course he's tired, stupid. He looks exhausted.

"Lieutenant made me eat some cookies from the vending machine. I'm just tired." Alex huffed out a sharp breath. "What's wrong? You smell weird. Like you're nervous."

"Thanks. You say the nicest things." Jason took him by the arm and tugged him toward the bed. "Probably too many things to hit me with at once. Being woken up to see you all beat up and tell me some half-crazed vamp has been gnawing at you."

"Now you smell angry."

Jason wrapped his arms around Alex to give him a hard squeeze. "I can't help how I smell. Try not to read too much into confused reactions when someone's half-asleep."

A little sneeze got their attention—Audacity, pawing at the covers and staring at the two of them as if they'd lost their minds.

"We're coming, your majesty." Jason decided to lead by example instead of trying to move Mt. Alex and climbed into bed, taking his spot by the wall. "There. Happy?"

Of course, she wasn't until Alex lay down with them, pulling the sheet up to his waist. She regarded the arrangement critically, let out a snort that was way too much like one of her dad's and settled in a kitten ball at the foot of the bed.

"Audacity has spoken," Jason murmured against Alex's shoulder.

The only thing he got back was a sleepy grunt. No sex of any kind was on the horizon that night and again Jason wondered why Alex hadn't just gone home to sleep. Maybe he felt guilty? Maybe the vampire feeding had been disturbing and he wanted some normal, plain humaning for a while?

And maybe you should stop running on the hamster wheel, brain. He might have just had a vampire but he came straight to you after. Shut up and go to sleep.

* * * *

"Mom." Jason fought a sigh. "You don't need it changed every three thousand miles."

"I read it online. You can't trust what mechanics say."

"Wait. Don't you think if a mechanic wanted to lie to you, that they'd say that you needed to change the oil more not less?"

She huffed into the phone. "You're supposed to be taking care of this."

"I am. I have been. If you check the log book I put in your glove box—"

"Maybe I'm getting old but I'm not senile yet. Your log says it's been three thousand miles since the last oil change."

Jason thumped his head against the wall. This wasn't an argument he had any chance of winning. "Okay. How about some time on Sunday?"

"You can't do it tonight?"

"Mom, Alex is here." The second it was out of his mouth, he knew it was the wrong thing to say. *Oh, God. Here it comes.*

After a moment's glacial silence, his mother whisper-hissed, "I see. Somehow this Alex is more important than your family now."

"No. He's not." *Though he doesn't expect me to drop everything and come running for things that can wait.*

Alex waved frantically from the kitchen doorway. Crap. He'd probably heard every word.

Jason covered the mouthpiece. "What, babe?"

"I don't mind. I'll go with you."

"Not really the point. She shouldn't be doing this."

The Alex frown he received was nearly thunderous.

"But she's your mom."

Now there's an unexpected alliance, Alex and my mom ganging up on me. Jason planted a quick kiss on Alex's cheek and put the phone back up to his ear. "I'll be there in a few minutes. Alex and I. Could you put your car in the drive so I'm not doing it in the street this time?"

Another huff. "What difference does it make?"

"Just do that one thing for me, Mom. Please."

She grumbled but acquiesced and Jason turned to his too-helpful lover. "She really doesn't need it done, you know."

"I...yeah." Alex stared at his feet. "But she was getting mad. And if you didn't go over, she'd blame me. And...she's your mom."

Pack. Fitting in with the pack. Those things were so real for Alex still and Jason hated that his family had made him so anxious about their possible rejection of him. As far as Alex was concerned, he was the outsider wolf coming out of the deep woods, cautiously circling the established family to see if he could convince them that he was acceptable.

Just another reason he'd be happier with someone else. *Stop it, stop it, stop it.*

"You're sure?" He waited for Alex's nod. "Okay. It shouldn't take long. But you know you're putting yourself in the line of fire, right?"

That didn't ease any of the frown lines even a fraction. "I can help. It'll go faster."

When they got to his parents' house, Mom had at least moved her Mercedes into the drive. She wasn't anywhere in sight as they unloaded tools and oil from the back of Jason's truck but she must have been watching from a window since she swooped out of the house just as Jason was getting ready to knock.

"Here." She held out her keys without greeting either of them. "Also, there's a noise in the back."

"What kind of noise?" Jason asked with what he felt was saintly patience.

"A squeaky noise when I turn. Could you look at that?"

He didn't point out that she might have mentioned it on the phone and he knew better than to interrogate further. "I'll take it around the block and see if I hear it. But this is probably something you should take to the shop."

"Why can't you fix it?"

"Like I said, I'll take a listen but I'm not a mechanic, Mom."

She shot a hard look at Alex, who stood back, uncomfortable and trying to pretend he wasn't listening, before she turned and stalked back to the house, muttering something that sounded like, "Not much of anything."

Jason did his best not to react, not to let Alex see. The issues with his family might quiet down eventually, but would Alex want to stick around that long? Did he really have enough reason to go through this aggravation?

His parents left them in peace while Jason worked and Alex was the perfect car maintenance companion, not distracting with extraneous conversation, handing over the right tools when asked. He'd probably helped his dad with this stuff. Only when Jason was finishing up and asked Alex for something that wasn't a tool did he balk.

"Could you go inside and ask Mom where she put the new oil filters I got her?"

Alex looked as if Jason had asked him to go face a horde of rabid squirrels riding starved crocodiles. "Me?"

"Please? My hands are covered in grease and you'd save me the trouble of cleaning up so I can get dirty again."

"Um. Okay."

"Thanks, hon. Appreciate it."

Alex squared his shoulders, his expression as determined as if he were going into battle with those previously mentioned squirrels. Good for him to face awkward social situations? Maybe. But Jason found he was second-guessing himself with everything Alex related.

The Shens' house was beautiful. Not huge and intimidating like Carrington's parents' house or even perfectly manicured like Krisk's. The beauty came from all the warm colors and all the light from windows and open rooms. It might have been welcoming if he'd felt welcome.

He found Jason's mom in the breakfast nook tucked away at the back of the kitchen.

"Ma'am, I'm sorry to bother you. Jason..." He faltered when she turned to glare at him. "Oil filters. He, um, wanted to know where they are."

"They're in the garage. By the snowblower. Jason will know." Her mouth twisted into an unhappy line as she continued to stare him down from a full foot below his height. "You're going to break his heart."

"Ma'am?"

"You're going to realize he's not enough for you and you'll leave him. Not that he should be with you, anyway. He should find a good, steady girl and settle down. Have a real family instead of one of pets other people threw away."

"Ma'am, I'd never —"

"You will. You should do it soon so it's not as hard for him. Just go back to your life being an important special police officer and leave my poor Jason alone."

He stammered and tried hard to get a sentence out, but it came out garbled. Instead, he shook his head and retreated. What was he supposed to say in the face of so much venom? He couldn't think of anything that wasn't rude or might start an argument and he was certain arguing with your boyfriend's mother was not a thing humans were supposed to do.

What *was* he supposed to do? If Jason's mother hated him, wanted him gone, the rest of his family would never truly accept him, even if Lisa and Julia had been nice. He wasn't going to leave Jason just because his mom thought Alex might hurt him in the future, but a terrible ache gnawed at his gut that Jason would be convinced to leave him before long.

He wouldn't be the one starting that conversation but an icy spike had wedged under his heart with the sudden certainty that it was inevitable.

Chapter Eight

The day of the wedding, Jason found he'd been conscripted. At least it meant he didn't have to wear a jacket and tie, which he appreciated. He wasn't a complete novice when it came to Indian-American fusion weddings, but because Kash's mom had insisted on a groom's *baraat* procession and since there were two grooms, everybody got to participate. Except the vampires, who were safely tucked inside the venue with some of the older guests and the officiants.

Also appreciated, no unhappy frightened horse or worse, elephant, had been pressed into service to carry the grooms. That left palanquins and the grooms' friends and relatives to carry them. Team Kyle consisted of his brothers, an uncle, Amanda, Jeff and Krisk, carrying a dapper Kyle in his cream tuxedo. His fiancé had two uncles, Alex, Vance, Greg and Jason.

And Kash? Looked like absolute royalty in a *sherwani* coat of soft blue with an embroidered white floral pattern and peacock blue *churidar* pants. One of Kash's aunts, beaming and laughing, wound a matching blue stole around each of his palanquin-bearers' necks while Kyle's bearers received gold ones from his aunt.

Guests chattered around them, greeting, hugging, gathering behind the three drum players.

"So, what do we do here?" Jason leaned in to ask Kash.

Kash's smile was more open and excited than he'd ever seen. "The drum leader will explain. When they start playing the *dhol* — "

"The dolls?" Vance asked, his eyes wide with overwhelmed panic.

"*Dhol*. The cylindrical drums. They play both ends. Once they start, you pick up the platform." Kash patted his colleague's shoulder. "Just follow along. You can't do anything *wrong* except drop me. Please don't do that."

"Are we taking bets?" Amanda called over from the other group. "Who drops a groom?"

There was some ribbing and catcalling back and forth until Alex's mom put a stop to it, telling them they should be ashamed while she tried desperately to smother a smile.

The drums began, Alex did a three-count and Kash's palanquin wobbled into the air. They had an unsteady moment with everyone's different heights, but they sorted out how to carry quickly and set off behind the guests. Kyle's did a little better since only Krisk was taller than the others and he simply shifted his corner to one hand to compensate. Some of the guests were leery of him but the extended families had obviously been briefed and accepted him with only a curious glance here and there.

The guests wore everything from suits to saris, though bright colors far outnumbered dark as the procession danced *bhangra* down the sidewalk, some more obviously practiced than others. That was fine, too. The point was joy and the majority of the guests understood. Toward the front of the crowd, even Mia Dunfee danced. She did it *seriously*, of course, as she did everything Jason had ever seen her do, but she still danced.

They set the grooms down in front of the Academy, rather than trying to navigate the steps to the front door. Kyle and Vikash took the stairs together to greet their parents gathered in the doorway in what appeared to be a blessing from each set of parents to the opposite groom. Once they went inside, brothers and uncles rushed after them and the guests began to file in.

Alex tucked his mom's hand into the crook of his elbow and reached for Jason on the other side. He was smiling as he said, "That was fun. Weddings should all have drums and dancing processions."

"Definitely better than having to sit through Pachelbel's *Cannon* yet again," Miriam chuckled.

Inside, flower garlands wound around the columns and the bannisters. Swags of them festooned the gallery railings above, explosions of bright yellow, orange and red. Alex closed his eyes and breathed deep on an unmistakably happy sigh while Jason collected programs for them. God, it was good to see Alex relaxed and enjoying himself. He looked gorgeous in the gray dress pants that molded perfectly to his ass and the dark green button-down that brought out the hint of green in his gray eyes.

The Academy's entrance hall was always stunning with its sweeping staircases, the gold and blood-red wallpaper and the huge, cathedral style windows. With all the flowers and brightly clothed guests? Luminous.

Following the other guests, they made their way to the upstairs galleries overlooking the lobby and second floor landing where the—Jason consulted his program—*mandap* was set up. The structure, a bright pavilion, was a work of art in itself with red and white tassels and silver stars hanging from the interior roof.

"He looks like a fairytale prince, doesn't he?"

The voice beside Jason's ear made him twitch. "Hey, Carr. Didn't see you there."

Carrington laughed, covering his mouth with the back of his hand to hide the fangs. "Easy to fade into the background here." He nodded to the couple ascending the stairs. "But this is breathtaking."

Something wistful had crept into his voice along with the wonder. *You, too, Carr? Is this going to start a marriage cascade?*

"It's amazing and Kash does look more like a god than usual."

Carrington half-turned away and let out a volley of sneezes. "Erf. It's all quite lovely but so many flowers are becoming an issue."

"Maybe you should tour the galleries then, Officer Loveless. Just until the ceremony is over." Valbuena was suddenly there, peering over Alex's shoulder. "Officer Wolf doesn't seem bothered."

Damn vampires and their stealth superpowers.

Alex snorted. "Oh, I'm bothered, sir. I'll be sneezing in a couple here. But it's nice. Like being outside."

"Good afternoon, ACO Shen. Or do I call you Jason in this setting?" Valbuena glanced down at Alex's hand twined with Jason's and frowned.

Yeah, that's how it is, Detective. At least for now. "Jason's fine. Have you met Alex's mom?"

"No. How insufferably rude of me." Valbuena narrowed his eyes at Jason before turning his most charming smile on Miriam. "Ma'am, I'm Detective Captain Richard Valbuena, currently on loan from State Paranormal."

Miriam offered a hand. "Dr. Miriam Tudosz. We have met, Captain. Briefly. When Alex was going through evaluation at State. You were lost in thought, looking out of a window at the rhododendrons. We talked about butterflies."

"I should remember that." He bowed over Miriam's hand. "My apologies. I'm perfectly monstrous."

"Not at all. Now hush, boys. They're starting."

Jason had to wrestle down one laugh at Miriam talking to the big bad vamp captain like he was three, then another when Erasmus limped up to join them and wrap his arms around Carrington. Valbuena's expression had turned sour, as if Carrington somehow didn't deserve someone who loved him.

Two officiants stood in front of the *mandap* — a Hindu priest in saffron and a Unitarian minister in a coral-colored suit and white stole, both barefoot. The parents sat beneath the canopy in white chairs on either side of a pair of embroidered hassocks. While this wasn't going to be a traditional wedding for either side of the family, Jason suspected they were trying to fuse all the important parts.

Pandit Bhat faced Kyle and Kash, who waited patiently on the wide steps scattered with flower petals, and began with the *Ganesh Puja*, the invocation of the god Ganesh to ask for the removal of all obstacles in the couple's path. Then all four parents came forward to help the *Navagraha Puja*, with the nine grains offered to the celestial deities.

Jason was sure he saw Kash's hand in the writing of the program—clear, concise and complete. He didn't feel lost at all. Rev. Myers came forward then to offer a blessing in Gaelic and the parents formally greeted their sons. When the grooms took off their shoes to enter the *mandap*, Kash's sisters, two dark like their mother, one blonde like their father, rushed forward and carried off Kyle's shoes, accomplished with a good deal of laughter from the sisters and a mock-glare of outrage from Kyle.

"Why did they do that?" Alex whispered as he scanned his program with a frown. Shoe theft hadn't been included.

Carrington leaned across Jason. "It's all in fun. Kyle has to pay them to get the shoes back or he can't leave the *mandap*. I'm surprised Kyle's siblings didn't retaliate."

He'd spoken too soon, of course, since two of Kyle's brothers ran in from the other side and snagged Kash's sandals.

"All's fair in love and wedding shoes," Erasmus said with a snicker.

The giggling and good-natured insult tossing between the siblings quieted, though the smiles remained as Vikash and Kyle took their places on the hassocks. Rev. Myers stood to the side so she didn't block the guests' view and took the grooms through their first set of vows and the exchange of rings, Kyle's voice shaking nearly to pieces on his *I do*.

"Give me a sec," Kyle murmured after the rings. Several relatives were wiping their eyes as Kyle ferreted out a tissue and tried to compose himself. Kash held his free hand, serious but patient as Kyle hiccupped and snuffled.

The concerned silence must have woken Audacity, napping in Miriam's oversized handbag. She stuck her head out to peer at what was happening, more adorable than usual in her headband with its big red bow.

Mii-rriiw?

Their position on the gallery and the museum's acoustics caused the chirping meow to bounce and echo wildly in the near-silence.

Kyle glanced up and laughed, wiping at his eyes and waving to them as he called up, "Thanks, Audi! Perfect timing!"

Laughter rippled through the guests as Kash leaned in to give his nearly-husband a quick hug. Then Pandit Bhat returned to them with a garland of golden flowers for each, which they held while they faced each other.

Into the hush that followed, Kash spoke softly, though the sound system picked it up. "You are my heart. You are my home. You are my lamp in the dark. Everything I am is yours, now and always."

If the unflappable Vikash Soren's voice wavered a little, and if his eyes glittered a little too brightly, no one remarked on it. He settled the garland over Kyle's head and leaned in to kiss his cheek.

Kyle gave him a crooked grin. "Killing me here, Kash."

"Sorry."

"It's okay. Since I'm about to destroy you."

Jason leaned in to whisper in Alex's ear, "Competitive wedding vows. I didn't realize that was a thing."

One corner of Alex's mouth ticked up. "You should see them playing video games."

Kyle drew in a deep, dramatic breath and began. "When I met you, I was half a person and didn't even know it. You understood my quirks, my fears. You laughed at my jokes. Most of the time."

He stopped and let the quiet laughter murmuring through the guests die down. "We fit together. Nothing had ever felt so right. For you, I wanted to be braver. For you, I wanted to be better. I wanted to erase every awful thing that ever happened. I wanted to keep giving you little gifts of good moments until the sadness in your eyes that's only there when you think no one's looking — until that went away. In nothing flat, you went from being the annoying, perfect statue I got saddled with to my heart, my home, my everything. Now and always."

Kyle managed to get Kash's garland over his head before Kash buried his face against Kyle's neck, shoulders shaking. They clung together while someone cut the sound for a few moments. When it came back, Kash's father was speaking, asking the guests to join them at the reception.

"That was amazing." Jason swallowed against the lump in his throat. "Wow. Do you want to mingle a little or head over to Bartram's?"

"I, um…" Alex's head swiveled between Jason and Captain Valbuena.

"Officer Wolf…Alex," Valbuena purred. "Has offered to drive my transport."

Damn it, Alex. I know you feel like you're responsible for him but this isn't work. "Okay?"

"Could you…" Alex squeezed his hand, eyes pleading. "Could you, um, take Mom and Audacity? Me and Krisk, we'll manage the transport box and meet you there?"

"All right." Jason patted Alex's chest. *He'll have Krisk there. It's fine.* "Not a problem."

"You're sure?"

Jason narrowed his eyes. "I'm sure. Don't make it sound like it's such a burden to hang out with your mom."

"I wasn't—"

Miriam disentangled herself from her son. "Go on, Alex. I'm sure transportation logistics take a bit. We'll start down. Say hello to some people and make our way over slowly."

Alex looked a little stricken but he bent to kiss Audacity's head and followed the captain, looking back over his shoulder every few yards.

"No, absolutely not." Carrington held up both hands when Jason glanced toward him. "I'm not getting involved."

"With what?" Jason tried for nonchalant and probably failed.

"Come on," Erasmus tugged on his vampire's arm. "Help me with the stairs."

They were whispering to each other as they made their way through the crowd, though Jason thought he heard *I wasn't going to* and *before you stir up trouble.*

"You look worried," Miriam prodded as they made their way to the stairs.

"Me? No. Why would I be worried?"

"Maybe you're worried for Alex's safety?"

Jason glanced down at her, trying to read something in her steady gaze. "I guess a little. But I know Alex can handle himself."

"I see."

Far too much meaning charged those two little words. "Miriam…"

"He loves you, you know." She squeezed his arm. "And you understand him better — you make more of an *effort* to understand him than anyone else he's had a relationship with."

"I know." Jason turned his attention to the stairs to avoid a misstep, not to avoid her eyes. "Thing is, I've never been jealous, never got upset if a lover had other things going on. This feeling I have now? It disturbs me."

"Hmm." Miriam held onto her long skirt to keep it from tangling with her boots. "Forgive me if I analyze, but I think there are three things happening here. The first is that Alex isn't built for juggling multiple partners. Wolves just aren't wired that way and you know that, which worries you. You're worried that Alex is working up to leaving you. The second is that you do *not* like Captain Valbuena, nor do you trust him."

"Crap. I didn't realize it was that obvious. And third?"

"You haven't talked to Alex about how insecure you're feeling."

"Damn it, Miriam. You're not supposed to know me this well already."

She shrugged. "You have enough early morning breakfasts with a person when their defenses are down, you learn some things."

His laugh wasn't entirely comfortable but he couldn't argue any of her points. He'd put off talking about certain things since just navigating a relationship with Alex had posed its own challenges. Really there weren't any excuses anymore, except cowardice.

By silent mutual agreement, they dropped the subject and spent the drive over to Bartram's Gardens talking about the ceremony and the families. They played a short game of *I think I saw this person or that person* and they exchanged stories of family wedding disasters.

He didn't return to the topic of Alex or vampires until they were parking at the beautiful Bartram's grounds. "Why was Valbuena at the wedding, anyway? Doesn't everyone resent him?"

"Mia brought him as her guest." Miriam waved a hand at his surprised sound. "Not that they're together. But she told me it was rude to exclude him."

"Oh. That makes sense. Do you talk to Lieutenant Dunfee, ah, often?"

"We don't chat on the phone every week, but we've spoken enough over the years to be social."

Jason took her arm to help her navigate a gravel pathway, letting that cover his shock. He hadn't thought the lieutenant was social with anyone.

Signs pointed them toward Eastwick Hill, which on the map looked like a bit of a hike. Golf carts waited in a patient row, drivers ready to assist, but Miriam rejected the idea.

"It's a perfect evening. We can see a little of the gardens while we walk."

"They're your heels," Jason said with a laugh. "Audacity, you should keep your head down. I don't think wolf cubs are allowed here normally."

Miw. Her answer was little more than a peep as she sank back into the depths of Miriam's bag. It really was a shame that she didn't get to see. Walking let them take in some of the historic parts — it was the oldest botanic garden in the country — and catch glimpses of the old house and barn. Strange, though. Jason felt an itch between his shoulder blades during the whole walk, as if someone might be watching. He peered around once or twice and there were other people, of course, but no one paying particular attention to them.

No. It wasn't other guests. It was more a feeling of the shrubs having eyes. *Weird.* He put it down to his being generally unsettled that day and tried to concentrate on being a good companion instead. Miriam knew plants, though she was better with animals, and they amused each other by identifying birds they saw along the way.

The new pavilion hove into view around a bend, its curved roof and airy construction reminiscent of a large estate's fanciful greenhouse, shining gold and white in the early evening sun. The transport box nestled over to one side already, so Alex had beaten them there after all. With the vampire. Who was now inside with Alex. *Stop it.*

Dozens of round tables for six with alternating orange and red tablecloths dotted the pavilion. A parquet dance floor interrupted the flow of tables at the far end. An attendant greeted each new guest at the entrance with a seating chart to ensure everyone found their seats. Much appreciated since Jason hadn't looked forward to searching the sea of tables for their name cards. Carrington's name card was on their table, as well as Erasmus' and Amanda's, which gave Jason a moment's social pause.

"Where did they put Krisk?"

Miriam stood on her tiptoes for a visual search, though she didn't gain much height by it. "To the right. With LJ."

Interesting. If LJ and Hunter had been at the wedding, Jason had missed them, though they were good at hiding and could've been anywhere. Here they sat out in the open, as much as two coats could be said to sit, in chairs to Krisk's left with Tim's house propped in a decorative box on the chair to the right. Jason squinted, unsure. Yes. Tim sat proudly atop his house wearing a spiffy top hat in place of his police hat and beyond him…

Alex stood chatting with Valbuena and a couple Jason didn't recognize. Rather, the vampire chatted. Alex stood there, shifting from foot to foot.

"Rescue?" Miriam suggested.

"Looks like I'd better. But I hate to abandon you."

Miriam prodded his arm. "Go on. Audacity's with me and I see Amanda on her way. We won't be alone long."

Girding his social loins, Jason worked his way over, stopping here and there to say hello and shake hands with people he knew or knew he should. Behind his mirror sunglasses, Valbuena tracked him all the way across the pavilion, maybe to unnerve him. *Sorry, pal. You're nothing compared to my grandmother.*

"Hey, babe." Jason slipped his hand into Alex's when he reached the group. Territorial, challenging and completely blatant? Yeah. Not his usual way of dealing with things, but this wasn't a usual day.

Alex leaned in to him, just enough to lend Jason his warmth. *Cue the warm fuzzies.* He squeezed Alex's hand and tried to keep up with introductions. *Nope. Lost every name already.*

"Your mom's looking for you," Jason said with the brightest smile he could muster. "Was nice to meet you folks. Richard, good to see you made it safely."

Credit where credit was due, Valbuena pulled out a charming return smile and a polite nod as Jason led his wolf away. For his part, Alex seemed relieved. *Good.*

Erasmus had just arrived with Carrington, who was folding up a bright blue parasol.

"Weren't there any golf carts left?" Amanda eyed the fancy umbrella critically.

Carrington hung it on the back of his chair with meticulous care. "There were. We wanted to take in the gardens, thank you very much, and I wasn't about to rush."

"It took some convincing." Erasmus didn't even try to hide a smirk. "Carr picks the strangest times for vanity. He couldn't get past the image of a big bad vampire Mary Poppins."

"All the vamps in *The Nightmare Before Christmas* had them," Alex pointed out.

A guilty spark of triumph flared in Jason's chest since it had only taken Alex thirty seconds back with his mom and his friends to stop fidgeting and join the conversation. *Back where you belong, big guy.*

Carrington heaved a dramatic sigh. "That was for comedic effect, you know. Regardless, it was nice to stroll in the sunshine without becoming dizzy. Not a practical solution while on duty, but convenient for off-hours." He shot a quick glance over at Valbuena. "For those of us who don't need to be transported like a crate of potatoes, at any rate."

"He's not that bad," Alex mumbled as he stared at the tablecloth.

"It can't be easy," Miriam added before anyone could jump on Alex's statement. "Dealing with vampire society in the first place and being put in charge of a department of vampires on top of it. I'd imagine his days are often a frustrating maze of egos."

Carrington put his chin on his fist as he regarded her. "You do realize not even my own mother can make me feel so mean and immature in so few sentences."

"Your mother has different priorities." Miriam took a quick glance around. "I suppose I could let Audacity out now, don't you think?"

Alex reached over and took the bag from her lap. He leaned over the top, calling softly, "Hey, sweetie, want to come out and see everyone?"

The red bow attached to a kitten head popped out, Audacity frantically chirp-purring and pawing at the air to be picked up. She settled in ladylike fashion on her dad's lap, seeming to take to heart his warnings about not wandering off, though it was only five minutes before she abandoned his lap for Jason's, then his for Carrington's, and so on.

The wedding party arrived soon after to cheers and applause. Kash had recovered his reserve and poise, though his smile flashed more teeth than usual. Kyle had already shed his tuxedo's jacket and tie, practically skipping with glee before he was even offered a glass of champagne.

They were *happy*, and while a tiny cauldron of anger bubbled inside Jason that marriage was the only societally respected and accepted relationship dynamic, he couldn't in any way direct that at Kyle and Kash. *They're happy.*

Jason had Audacity back on his lap and Alex's hand in his when the champagne came around. He didn't need the bubbly either to feel like he'd taken a big sip of happy. Content. A warm dose of family, even if Valbuena lurked on the other side of the room. He was here in the glowing heart of Alex's love that he extended like a sheltering roof over those he considered his.

Dinner was also more interesting that most wedding dinners Jason had been to. Each table had a lazy susan instead of a centerpiece and instead of the servers bringing each guest a plate, they brought a tray of various dishes to place on the carousel. He was more accustomed to seeing this arrangement at traditional Chinese banquets—joyfully surprising. The food offerings also followed the fusion theme with curries—madras, tikka, vindaloo—alongside sliced roast beef and colorful salads.

Audacity mewed at Jason to excuse herself and returned to her dad, who made sure she got a portion of roast beef cut into tiny pieces before he served himself. Over at Krisk's table, the coats didn't eat, though, they seemed to be acting out a story using silverware, while Krisk cut up leafy greens and placed them on a bread plate for Tim. There may have been some guests looking askance at their table, but none of the non-humans paid attention. Besides, how cute was a fuzzy purple ovoid who managed to keep his top hat on while he devoured his tiny salad?

Good food, good conversation, a little bit of misty-eyed warm and fuzzy when Kyle and Kash had their first dance—everything was perfect. Until the dancing had progressed past the obligatory ones with the grooms and family members, and Detective Captain Richard Valbuena decided to bring his perfect vampire self to their table.

"I hope you're enjoying the evening." Valbuena gave the table a military bow, mostly directed toward Miriam. He looked good in his tailored gray suit with his blond hair loose around his shoulders. Not the type Jason would've gone for, but there was no denying he rated high on the hotness scale.

"Alex." His hand went to his heart, his entire demeanor one of gentle pleading. "Would you consider honoring me with a dance?"

Half turned in his chair, Alex froze. "Um…I don't…it's a…a waltz?"

"No need to know how." Valbuena's smile turned bright and encouraging. He held out a hand to Alex. "I'll lead."

I'll just bet you will. Jason kept his mouth shut, though he wanted to smack the captain for making Alex uncomfortable. But this was part of the deal, that he let Alex work through things on his own even though every cell in Jason's brain was screaming *no!*

"Um…" Alex gave Audacity to his mom, though she complained about her displacement. Then he was standing and giving the captain his hand while Jason's heart sank into his shoes and he wished he hadn't eaten quite so much.

"Jason." Miriam leaned over Alex's empty chair. "It's just a dance."

"Right," Jason rasped out, gulping champagne to cover the sandpaper demon that had stolen his voice.

Of *course* Valbuena had perfect dance posture as he put his hand at Alex's waist and positioned Alex properly. Of *course* he didn't so much dance as glide and float, his steps flawless even when Alex stumbled. Of *course* he was just commanding enough and just gentle enough that it worked and Alex picked it up quickly. And *damn* him. He looked too genteel and beautiful in motion to be real. People watched the two of them with longing, with hunger.

Alex looked like someone had hit him between the eyes with a slab of concrete. Poleaxed, that was the word, as if he couldn't figure out how he was moving in time to the music. His own natural grace and his hunter's ability to anticipate movement made it all look effortless after the first missteps. What would've taken Jason hours to learn, Alex absorbed into his muscle memory in moments.

They have so much in common. Physically, they're far closer to equals. Neither one is fully human. They're both cops. And Valbuena has no family to make Alex feel unwelcome. Damn it.

Jason was just wondering how awkward of him it would be to cut in when a shriek from the other side of the pavilion distracted him. A man, who had been standing behind a couple chatting with them, toppled as if someone had pulled his feet from under him. A woman three feet beyond him fell over not half a second later. Every police officer on the guest list rose from their tables and moved toward the disturbance before Jason could blink. Carrington beat them all to the stricken guests and while he was helping the woman up, asking her questions, he spotted something that made him hiss and display fangs.

God, what now? Jason made his cautious way toward the dance floor to have a better sight angle. If these were more hoax animals, he hoped they weren't ones with big teeth and claws. The tripoderos had been bad enough.

Movement caught the corner of his eye just before a *thing* barreled into him and knocked him flat. The brief glimpse he had as it vanished between the tables was of a circle, maybe three feet high, covered in…no, that was ridiculous.

Kyle's dad and Amanda had taken on the task of herding guests toward the exits, assuring everyone it was temporary, an animal had gotten into the pavilion.

Kash appeared at Jason's elbow to help him up and murmured close to his ear, "Hoop snake."

Scales. Yep. The circle of toppling had been covered in scales. "That's just great."

They retreated to the open space of the dance floor, back to back with Alex and Valbuena and Jason realized they were waiting for his direction. "Okay, there'll be two of them if the pattern holds. Since these aren't regular snakes, we don't know if they're venomous, so *don't* grab them barehanded. We don't have any grabbers or bags..."

LJ zipped up to them with a box of trash bags he must have snagged from the bar.

"Good thinking. Better than nothing. Everyone spread out to the edges. We'll work our way toward the center. Use a chair to lift tablecloths as you go. Don't risk a strike by using your hands. Or, ah, sleeves."

Not something the grooms should've been doing at their own wedding, but Jason figured he'd insult them by telling them not to take risks when their guests were. They fanned out, most of the 77th, himself and the captain. Amanda held the one entrance, watching for snake escapees, while Krisk held the other. Only Alex remained on the dance floor, head up, sniffing the air.

Jason began a careful, deliberate check from his chosen corner. Snakes liked *dark* and *under* when they wanted to hide, so he and LJ lifted the first tablecloth from either side, exposing under the table and all the chair seats at once. Nothing. Next one. They were three tables into their search when Jason heard the slide of something heavy against fabric. He turned, tapping LJ on the shoulder and pointing, just as one of the hoop snakes slithered off one of the chairs.

Instead of continuing its undulating course or pulling back to strike, this snake pulled itself into a straight line, whipped tail and head off the ground and took its tail in its mouth. Jason lunged for it, trying to bag it before it finished the contortions, but he was a hair too slow. It sped away in a rolling hoop behind the next table.

LJ signaled left with his sleeve, Jason went right with his bag wide open. As he rounded the table at a crouch and caught a glimpse of blue and yellow scales, the hoop snake puffed up like an inflating tire and charged LJ. He jumped back and spread his plackets wide, presumably to catch the snake with his own body as it charged. Good strategy in theory but the force of the collision knocked LJ to the floor, sleeves flailing as the hoop snake rolled over him.

A blur of dark green and shiny black buttons tore in from the side and wishboned the snake. Hunter beat at the snake's head with her sleeves, even though Jason had said not to, and provided the distraction necessary for Jason to pop the bag over the hoop snake and scoop it up.

Jason scrambled to his feet to take stock as Hunter helped LJ up. Across the room, Carrington had also ignored advice and had the second snake behind the head, lowering it carefully into the bag Shira held out for him. A quick glance around showed everyone up and only mildly disheveled. Except for three things.

Wolf and Krisk were gone, and so was Captain Valbuena.

Chapter Nine

Though the sun had set, Wolf had worried for the captain at first. But Valbuena kept his sunglasses on and only grew steadier as the light faded.

He'd caught the scent immediately, the ceramic dust scent of the small versions of the hoop snakes. Part of Wolf felt bad deserting the pavilion but he knew there were enough competent people to catch two snakes. This mystery thing, this ceramic duplicate in miniature, this impossibility was *not* getting away from him again. He'd caught sight of the two little hoop snakes lurking just outside the pavilion. When they took off, he'd followed through the gardens in the thickening dusk, first by sight then by scent.

By the time he'd reached Harley Avenue, Captain Valbuena had caught up to him, heaving and puffing, waving away Wolf's concern. Krisk messaged a bare minute later saying he was bringing the car, give him a direction.

South, Wolf sent back. *On Eastwick now.*

"Do you see it still, Alex?" the captain asked as they got moving again. At least he'd stopped wheezing.

"No."

"Then where are we going?"

"I still smell it, sir. It's not far ahead."

"How can you smell *anything* in this part of town?" The frustration in Captain Valbuena's voice made him sound much more predator than officer.

"I...wolf nose, sir. But we have to move."

That wasn't a problem for the captain. He kept up with Wolf like no one had ever been able to, running beside him even as Wolf vaulted fences and took open stretches at top speed. The ceramic snakes were still up ahead, though he couldn't seem to close the distance.

About halfway down Eastwick, the ceramics stopped following roads altogether. They dashed out into the broken fields and made a zigzagging circuit around the Watt Khmer Palelai, maybe afraid of people spotting them at the temple.

Out the temple gates and onto South 58th Street, Wolf started to wonder if they were going anywhere in particular at all. There wasn't anything down this way after the railroad tracks. Was there?

"There." Captain Valbuena gripped his arm and pointed, the cedar-vampire scent this close almost strong enough to throw Wolf off his ceramic animal trail.

Distracting, that smell. Made his heart into a pile driver against his breastbone. But he caught the flash of ceramic sheen as the little hoop snakes rolled over the tracks toward a ragged fence of mismatched materials. They hurried after them and turned the corner just in time to see the hoop snakes go up a ramp and into an odd little house, one that Wolf could have sworn shouldn't have been there. He sent a hasty text to Krisk—

End of S 58. House past the RR tracks.

No house occupies that ground.

Does now. Come meet us.

Ten minutes. Informed Jason of whereabouts. All is well there.

Guilt punched Wolf hard in the gut that Krisk had remembered to message Jason and he hadn't. "Approach, Captain, or wait for backup?"

Captain Valbuena tipped his head to the side in a gesture eerily like Carrington considering a scene.

"There is only one heartbeat inside that house."

Wolf gaped at him. "You hear that? Out here?"

"It's a rather specific adaptation, I will admit." Valbuena stared at the little house a moment, a twisting one story with strange bits of gingerbread trim stuck here and there along the rooflines. "Well, then. I suppose the polite thing to do is knock."

"Sir." Wolf dared to seize the captain's arm, though all he got for it was a raised eyebrow. "What if there's magic?"

Valbuena covered Wolf's hand with his own and gave a gentle squeeze. "You're not frightened of magic, are you?"

"Yes, sir." Wolf swallowed hard. "It's how I got like this."

"Ah, but you didn't have me. I have picked up a thing or two over the years. Come, Officer Wolf. Let's get to the bottom of this nonsense."

Captain Valbuena folded his sunglasses and slipped them into his jacket pocket as he retrieved his badge. His knock hovered between official police sharp and *hey, is this dog yours* inquisitive, of which Wolf approved. He hated to think about someone's mom being shocked out of her skin by a police knock.

After a few moments, a tiny eye-sized window opened in the door. An oak-brown eye peered out and a voice whispered, "Who's there?"

"Police, ma'am," Captain Valbuena responded gently, holding his badge up at eye-window level. "We need to ask you a few questions, please."

"You can't come in." The voice still whispered but had gathered force. "You're a vampire. Who's that with you?"

The captain blinked as the porch light turned on, obviously taken aback by the occupant knowing what he was and annoyed at having to wait for his eyes to adjust again. "This is Officer Wolf who's assisting m—"

"He needs to step into the light."

The captain turned to Wolf and shrugged with a little wave of his hand to invite Wolf forward. The door flew open abruptly.

"He's a *wolf!*"

A woman stood in the doorway, almost eye-to-eye with him, and he only had an impression of wild auburn curls and long limbs before he found himself seized by the shirtfront and dragged over the threshold. She took his face between her hands and searched his eyes.

"You are a wolf," she murmured. "But you can't go back now, poor cub. I'm years too late."

How does she know? How does she know any of it? "It's…um…I'm all right, ma'am. Being human."

"Patches, down," the woman admonished the patchwork dog before she pointed to the pom-pom cat and the paper crane in turn. "And that's Fluff. And that's Flap."

"This is all quite charming, ma'am," Captain Valbuena said from the doorway. "But could I please come in?"

"Mama said never to invite vampires inside."

"But he's…" Wolf was trying to keep up but found himself perplexed by someone who knew so much and seemed so childlike. He cleared his throat. "Can't you come in, Captain?"

"No. I quite specifically can*not* come in." Captain Valbuena clipped each syllable.

"Oh. Um. Ma'am? He really is a police officer."

"But he's a vampire."

"Yeah. He is. But he's one of the good guys. Promise."

She leaned around Wolf to squint at the captain. "All right, since a wolf speaks for you."

The hairs on the back of Wolf's arms stood up as she reached past him, that strange unnerving frisson he picked up with magic in play close by. Her hand shot out and closed over the captain's, rosewood against his milk white.

"*Taci*," she whispered, running her free hand over the doorframe as she pulled him forward into the house. "*Taci*."

The humming of magic stilled and the captain drew a slow breath. "Thank you. I'm Detective Captain Valbuena."

The woman gave him a smile so open and guileless that it somehow made her age harder to pinpoint. Somewhere between thirty and fifty was Wolf's best guess. She offered them each a curtsy with a swirl of her long flouncy skirt. "I'm Pecca Teecosi. How exciting to have visitors. Though a little scary, too."

"No need to be frightened, ma'am. Just a few questions. I don't suppose you'd mind spelling your name?"

She leaned over the captain's phone as she spelled it out for him, absently holding an arm up so the origami crane could come and perch.

"Do you live alone here, Ms. Teecosi?"

"What a silly question. Do all detectives ask such silly questions? Oh, maybe it's to lull people into thinking all the questions are ridiculous and then you *pounce*." She mimed one with a two-footed hop and a mock growl. "I shall play the game correctly, then. No, I have all my friends here."

"Um, do any other humans live here, ma'am?" Wolf ventured.

"No. I'm the only human here since Mama died." Her hands flew to her face. "Oh, my goodness! I'm being rude. Would you like some tea? Come in. Come in. You should call me Pecca. Since I quieted the wards for you and all."

She skipped—actually skipped—ahead of them. Captain Valbuena bent to examine Fluff, who sniffed at him in return, before he followed their hostess. Wolf took a moment to sort out the scents in the house, herbs and spices, recently made beef stew, old wood, dusty fabrics and, yes, ceramics.

When he reached the kitchen, the captain had taken a seat at the old-fashioned Formica table and Pecca was putting the kettle on.

"Would you like tea, Officer Wolf? Captain Vampire doesn't drink tea. I should've thought of that. But you might. I have chamomile if you don't like black tea?"

"That would be nice, ma'am. Thank you." He took the chair next to the captain, leaning in close to murmur, "I smell them."

"You smell who, Officer Wolf?" Pecca asked brightly as she rattled about in the cabinets.

Captain Valbuena put a warning hand on Wolf's arm. "Ms. Pecca, are you in the habit of adopting animated objects as pets?"

"Adopting?" She stared at him with a puzzled frown.

"Yes. The ones like Patches and Fluff."

"Oh. Heee. No." Pecca helped a tiny pipe cleaner elephant out of the fruit bowl. It trumpeted and trundled off down the counter. "I make them."

"All of them?"

The kettle whistled, so she didn't answer until she had tea ready for herself and Wolf. She came to join them at the table and tucked her feet up onto the chair to sip her tea. "Yes, all of them. I work in lots of materials."

"Do you, um..." Wolf took a polite sip of his tea. "Pottery? Do you do that?"

"I do! Do you want to see? I built my own kiln and everything."

Captain Valbuena patted the air with one palm. "Perhaps not just now. Did you happen to create a pair of animated hoop snakes?"

"Just a couple of weeks ago. Were those bad things outside?"

"They were." The captain gave a careful nod and set aside his notetaking on his phone. "Officer Wolf and I followed them here."

"That's how you found the house. I thought maybe the misdirection was failing." A sharp knock on the front door interrupted them. Pecca's hands flew about like drunken butterflies. "More visitors! What a night."

She leapt up and raced for the door, bare feet slapping against linoleum, then hardwood. After a moment, she shrieked, "Oh, my goodness! There's a giant lizard in a suit out there!"

"No need for alarm, Ms. Pecca," Captain Valbuena called out as he rose and made his way to her. "That's Officer Krisk. He's with us."

The door clicked open and Pecca called out, "Come in, Officer Lizard Person. Come in. Apparently we've been expecting you."

"You don't have to quiet the wards for Krisk?" Captain Valbuena asked in a tone that might have been a little offended.

"Of course not, silly. He's not a vampire."

Wolf peeked around the corner to find Krisk standing in the front hallway with his tail thumping a slow, bemused beat on the hardwood while Pecca examined one of his hands.

"I guess you could be…" she murmured as she traced a claw. "But you probably don't want me to say."

Krisk shook his head slowly.

"All right, Officer Lizard. Come on back. We're having tea. Some of us. Do you like tea?"

Captain Valbuena gave up his seat to Krisk in favor of leaning against the counter and once again they waited for the rituals of hospitality to be fulfilled.

"Could we see some of your pottery creations, Ms. Pecca?" the captain asked while she brought Krisk his green tea.

"Sure!" Pecca let out three sharp whistles through her teeth.

Wolf tensed, listening. Krisk had gone still and the captain had cocked his head so Wolf knew they heard it, too. Soft tick-tick-ticks approached from the hallway accompanied by a sound like someone rolling a can across the floor. Soon, the ceramic hoop snakes rolled into the kitchen, followed by a pair of ceramic jackalopes. The snakes un-hooped themselves and the jackalopes sat on their hind legs, all four of them regarding Pecca patiently.

"These visitors wanted to see you," she told them with a cheery wave. "You can touch them carefully but don't talk too loud or move too fast."

Wolf bent down as one of the jackalopes hopped over to him. In the bright light of the kitchen, with the ceramic animals standing still, he could make out the amazing details of fur and delicate antler prongs. The painted whiskers twitched and the black eyes even blinked at him as they studied each other.

"It's beautiful," he whispered.

"Thank you." Pecca picked up one of the foot-long snakes and let it twine around her fingers. "The ceramic ones are special."

"They are quite astounding." Captain Valbuena stayed where he was, arms crossed over his chest. "Are all of your pottery animals based on cryptids and hoax animals?"

"They are." She nodded enthusiastically. "I have this wonderful book."

"Could we perhaps see the book?"

Pecca frowned. "All right. It's a very special book. And Detective Vampire shouldn't touch it."

Wolf looked at her sharply. "Why not?"

"Because it has magic and he has magic but they're different flavors and I don't think they'd mix. Kind of like having chocolate and onion ice cream."

"Very well, Ms. Pecca. I'll keep back and won't touch." Captain Valbuena gave her a crooked smile. "Though I wonder if I'm the chocolate or the onion part."

"Probably onion," Pecca kept talking as she walked through the doorway into what looked like a messy den. "Don't take that wrong. Onions and chocolate are both great, of course. Just not together."

"Well put," the captain chuckled.

Pecca returned with a book larger than her head, art book sized, though this one looked old with its cover of red leather and gilt decoration. She placed it on the table with a heavy thud and Wolf scrambled to clear the teacups away so she could open it. The first page she leafed to had a beautiful painting of a pair of jackalopes, almost identical to the ceramic ones. The only text on the facing page was the word *Jackalopes* in fancy script. She turned to another page, this one showing the tripoderos in a field, one with legs telescoped and one with them collapsed.

Captain Valbuena broke the quiet in a reverent tone. "Quite beautiful. And the whole book? These fanciful, imaginary creatures?"

"Sure. Every page. I haven't made all of them yet. But I pick a new one every couple of months."

Wolf had a terrible feeling starting to gnaw at him. "Ms. Pecca? Have you had the book long?"

"Not so long. No. Let me think." She squinched up her nose while she stared at the ceiling. "It was summer. Maybe July. I don't keep track all the time anymore. Not since Mama died. But summer, definitely, and I went to expiditionise."

"Pardon?"

Pecca blew a wayward curl out of her eyes. "Goodness, it's pretty clear, Detective Vampire. I can't grow or make everything I need here. Couple times a year, I go out to the farmer's markets and such. An expedition."

"Ah, forgive me. Please go on."

"You're a very polite vampire. Mama said you were all rude and stuck-up."

Wolf did his best not to smile. He wasn't sure he managed.

"So, I was at a market and a man comes up to me when I'm buying...something. Probably herbs that don't grow in my garden. Funny. I don't remember. Anyway, he said he had something I'd be interested in and he gave me this book. Except we weren't in the market anymore. Where were we? Hmm. He had a car? A van, maybe? Huh. I guess I was *really* concentrating on the book. He showed me the pictures and told me how to think about the pictures so sculptures made from them would come alive. And they did!" She finished with a bright smile and a dramatic sweep of her hand at her creations.

Krisk typed something out on his phone and turned it so Wolf and Pecca could see.

Already proficient with animation. Book was needed?

"It's different with fired clay, Officer Lizard. I don't know how to explain it. I can animate regular clay, but that doesn't last long and it's sad. Once it'd been in the kiln and all hardened, though? Nope. Never worked. Until I got my book."

"What did the man look like? The one who gave you the book?" Captain Valbuena's question was friendly, polite, but it still sent a chill down Wolf's spine.

"He was…" She trailed off with a frown. "He was taller… No, maybe not. He had… You know, the only thing I can remember is he was wearing black. And he had magic tingles. Of course he did. He had the magic book and knew how it worked. I can always feel magic tingles, though."

Wolf shared a look with Captain Valbuena. *There's your connection, sir. Happy?* While the captain's eyes had taken on a predatory gleam, he didn't look pleased.

"Your ceramic companions, do they do anything?"

"Lots of things." Pecca's forehead wrinkled and she spoke slowly as if no longer sure of the captain's intelligence. "Hop. Roll. Walk. Fly. Run. Some of them like to sit with me."

Captain Valbuena cleared his throat. "Yes. I beg your pardon. I meant do they do anything magical."

"You really should've said that then. No. They're just like my other friends. They keep me company."

"Ms. Pecca." The captain pursed his lips, staring at his shoes a moment before he continued. "I'm about to tell you something that you might not find pleasant. We believe — we have reason for some certainty — that your ceramic friends are somehow creating life-sized, actual flesh and blood versions of themselves. These versions have been attacking people."

She snorted a laugh, then cut off on a gasp, staring at him. "You're serious. But that's insane and it just can't be. My creations don't work that way."

"Four times now, we have evidence that your creations were present at the scene of an assault." Captain Valbuena's voice remained soft but cold menace licked around the edges of his words. "Twice, officers have actually *seen* them at the scene. Ms. Teecosi, these larger versions of your creations have wounded an animal control officer. Assaulted a crowd at a charity event. Took down guests at a wedding reception. Attacked *children*."

"No." Pecca shook her head so violently that her curls obscured her face. "It's not possible. My friends wouldn't hurt anyone."

"Not only is it possible but it will happen again if we don't stop it." Captain Valbuena scooped the ceramic jackalopes off the floor. "I don't believe you had any malicious intent, but rather that you were manipulated. Whatever the case, these creatures are clearly dangerous and must be disposed of. We're going to need to confiscate them and ask you to accompany us to the station for a full report."

"You... You don't even have a warrant," Pecca snapped at him, static sparking and popping from her hair.

"Captain," Wolf said softly. "This might not —"

"I'm State Paranormal, Ms. Teecosi. I don't need a warrant for dangerous magical items."

The static became a crackling as Pecca's hair lifted from her head to wave like seaweed in a storm. Golden light shone from her eyes as she raised both arms toward the captain. Startled, he backpedaled, green light playing over his fingers. Whatever spell he tried to call, even Wolf could see it was too late.

Both jackalope ceramics vanished from his hands to reappear on the counter behind Pecca. A rumbling vibration ran through the floor as Pecca included all three of them in her widening arms.

"You will *not!*" Wind sighed and rattled through the kitchen as her voice rose to a shriek. "You will *not* hurt my friends! Go away! *Esci di qui!*"

On the last word, Wolf found himself lifted and hurled through the air so fast it blinded and deafened him. He landed so hard he bounced and skidded across a rough, unforgiving surface, blinking as he tried to get his sight to return. Something was burning. He hoped it wasn't him.

As he sat up, blurry shapes resolved into Krisk on his right and Captain Valbuena on his left, all of them sprawled on the pavement back out on the street. None of them smoldered, so the burning scent had to be from the explosion of magic needed to hurl the three of them out of the house. They hadn't gone far, still right in front of where Pecca's address was, but the house itself had vanished, leaving what appeared to be an empty lot garlanded with mist.

"How dare she?" the captain snarled as he pushed up to his feet. The green lights danced around his fingers again, gathering, growing as he stalked back toward the mist. "Magical assault of police officers."

"Sir, wait! Don't—"

Wolf winced when Captain Valbuena's confident stride ended in a flash and a crackling sizzle as he collided with the mist. He sailed through the air a second time to land at Wolf's feet.

Phone out, Krisk texted as he huffed out a hard breath.

Suit will require replacement.

"Yeah." Wolf tucked his phone back in his pocket. "Just hope the captain's in better shape than his jacket. I think we'd better box him up and leave Ms. Pecca alone right now."

Krisk nodded and limped over to open the back door of the transport truck. Just as Wolf crouched to gather the disheveled and magic-singed captain in his arms, a black object hurtled out of the mist at him. He ducked instinctively and winced when the object connected with Captain Valbuena's head where it broke in two.

"Oops. Your cell phone's toast, too, sir." Wolf tucked both pieces into the captain's inside suit pocket and lifted him gently. "Guess you left it on the counter in there. I'm not criticizing, sir, but you might want to rethink how you talk to her."

At least they knew the what and some of the how. The rest would have to wait until they could get back in that house.

Chapter Ten

"Should I check for bite marks?" Jason wanted to bite his tongue off the second he'd said it but he was exhausted and his mouth got away from him. The words had leapt out sharp and jealous.

"Jason, don't." Alex wilted against the doorway to toe off his dress shoes. The shirt in its perfect shade of green was gone, replaced by a ratty old sweatshirt with a Drexel logo. Alex's good pants had some odd scraped bare places at one hip and both knees.

"Sorry. I didn't mean—"

Alex waved the apology off. "We're both tired. Where's Mom?"

"I begged her to go to bed a while back. Told her I'd wait up for you."

"Audacity?"

"Went to sleep with your mom. She had a big day." Jason scrubbed both hands over his face. "You want a snack, shower or bed?"

Alex stared at his socks for so long, Jason wondered if he'd fallen asleep standing up. "I want to scrub my brain out and pretend these last couple weeks didn't happen."

"What happened out there?"

"We found where the hoax animals are coming from." Alex wandered to the kitchen and stuck his whole head in the fridge. When he emerged, he had the remains of a roast chicken that he set on the counter and started to rip pieces from, devouring and growling with every bite.

"That's good though, right? I mean, it's over now."

"S'complicated," Alex muttered around a savage bite. "What happened at the reception?"

Okay. Tired and frustrated so we're not talking about that right now. "Things settled down after your squad mates whisked the snakes away. Carrington managed to explain it to the guests like it was all perfectly normal rat snake behavior and no one had been in danger. Dr. Hayes said he'd never seen a rat snake that color but he laughed it off."

Alex raised an eyebrow, though he didn't slow his devouring. "Dr. Hayes was there?"

"He was. I didn't see him at the wedding, but I didn't see a lot of people. My bets are on Kash's mom inviting him as your squad's benefactor. Carrington's parents were there, too. It's kinda fun to watch him avoid them at a party. He's really good at it."

"Hrmm," Alex growl-agreed as he gnawed on a leg bone.

"Alex, don't bite on that. It'll splinter." Jason waited until Alex reached for a tumbler and started to drink glass after glass of water. "So the party went on. There was cake. Toasts, the usual things. Everything was fine."

"Good." Alex moved more slowly now, more deliberately as he replaced the plundered chicken in the fridge.

"Are you hurt?" Jason asked.

"A little bruised." Finally, Alex turned to meet his eyes. "Please don't freak out. They're just bruises."

"So anything less than a broken bone is no big deal, huh?" Jason wrapped his arms around Alex's waist.

"They just don't last long for me." Alex laid his head on Jason's shoulder with a sigh.

Jason caught his left wrist before Alex could hug him. Ragged puncture wounds marred the underside. "Christ. I thought you said he was being *careful*."

"She broke his hip the second time she threw him out." Alex pulled back, rubbing at the marks. "It was an emergency."

"She broke — *God*. Do you even hear yourself? You all act like you're indestructible. I mean, I guess Valbuena is, almost. Except that you have to keep rescuing him."

Alex pulled out a kitchen chair and sat hard. "He was doing his job. *I* was doing my job."

"I'm sorry. I know you were." Jason joined him at the table, pulling in slow, steadying breaths. "It's hard not to worry about your superhero boyfriend. Guess Valbuena's not as bad as you thought, huh?"

"He's, um…" Alex shrugged. "He's used to doing things his way. Having things his way. Makes him a little hard headed, maybe. Not always… It's not that he's rude. His manners. He just, um, maybe doesn't think that the thing he's saying might hurt somebody."

"But whatever happened tonight, he was putting himself on the line, wasn't he?"

A slow nod, then Alex put his head on his arms. "He's very brave. Smart. Puts things together fast. Probably one of those detectives who drives the top brass crazy. I can't see him ever giving up."

"And he's handsome and a great dancer," Jason added in a soft murmur. Bitterness reared its head again. *Seriously, how could I dream of competing with a vampire?* "Bet he'd be a fun date."

"Are you...?" Alex raised his head halfway, brow furrowed in confusion. "Is this a...? Are you breaking up with me?"

"No." Jason nearly flung himself across the table reaching for Alex's hand. *No, no, no, I'm scared to death about you breaking up with me.* "Alex, no. I'm doing this wrong. I'm doing everything really badly because it's late and it was stupid to start any serious conversation now."

"You can't *not* explain now. I'll worry about this all night."

"I'm not breaking up with you. I'm not trying to push you away. It's just... I worry. A lot. That I'm not enough for you. That one day soon you'll see that and that maybe Valbuena or someone like him's more the someone you need."

"I've never thought that." Alex pulled his hand away, his eyes searching Jason's face restlessly.

"All I'm saying is that I've seen how he looks at you. I'm trying my best to stop being insecure about him being a superhero like you but I can see how it could happen between you. Especially since you spend so much time with him."

Alex made a strangled sound as he staggered up from the table. "I don't want anyone but you. I wouldn't..."

"I'm just making you upset. Look, I love you. I do. And I'm *not* leading up to a break up conversation here. It was a dumb time to bring up something complicated." *Oh, God, was it ever dumb since now you're thinking about it.* "I'm going home so I don't say anything else to make things worse. Let you get some sleep."

Alex surged forward and caught him in a crushing hug before he could get two steps from his chair. "I love *you*. I don't—" He choked on the last word, too obviously close to breaking down.

"I know, babe. I know." Jason hugged him back, rocking them both. "I love you, too. You know that, right? I've never loved anyone so hard before. There's so much of it, I think my heart's gonna shatter sometimes. Little gross pieces of Jason heart all over the floor."

The sound he got for that might've been a laugh.

"Go sleep. Call me tomorrow when you have a chance. Meet me for lunch maybe if you have time. It'll be okay. I'm sorry."

"Okay," Alex whispered before lifting his head and seizing Jason's lips in a desperate, bruising kiss. "Okay."

He went upstairs. Jason let himself out the front door. Outside a cricket chirped in solitude. A dog barked far away. Solitary things, and he was one of them tonight. Jason felt as if his heart was truly breaking. If he had just managed to ruin this, what he and Alex had, it would never be whole again.

* * * *

Guzzling coffee Monday morning to try to clear the heavy cobwebs, Wolf had already finished the large whatever it was that Jeff had brought him and was trying Larry's coffee. Awful, of course. Could strip wallpaper, probably. But he needed something horrible to yank him out of his stupor. He hadn't called Jason on Sunday. He should have but he'd been in a fog, unable to process what had happened the night before. Now here he was, at work, with everyone tiptoeing around him, even Kyle and Kash, who were apparently putting off a honeymoon until after the end of the year. No matter how he sorted through the conversation, it had sounded like Jason was trying to find an excuse to break up with him. Maybe his family had said things. More things. Made Jason feel so bad...not that it mattered.

Jason was going to leave him.

Larry stopped whistling, a container of powdered creamer halted waist high in the air indicating where he was. Wolf had the uncomfortable impression that Larry was staring at him in shock.

"What?"

The creamer tipped sideways and up in what was obviously a ghost shrug. Wolf had no answer for questions he couldn't even guess at, so he growled at Larry and poured another cup.

"Officer Wolf? Hey, are you okay?" Eva stood beside him, eyeing him warily.

Say something reassuring. Say something polite. "Why?"

Despite his snarl, her frown just deepened. "Because your aura's all...dark. Like your woodland friends are scared to come out and your books are all about depressing things."

"Oh." Wolf put down the cup, the backs of his eyes stinging. "Um. Excuse me."

He made it to the men's room before the stinging ran over into tears and there he stood with both hands gripping the sink as they fell with little *plip-plip* splashes onto the chipped ceramic. *Stupid, stupid, stupid.* Jason had said they weren't breaking up but this was how it always started, with Wolf not being able to grasp something simple for humans. Despite Jason's reassurances that they would talk, sleep hadn't come for the past two nights, so now Wolf was exhausted, more upset than he should be and unable to catch himself. He tried gripping the sink harder but it just hurt his hands. Then he made the mistake of catching a glimpse of his miserable, tear-stained face in the mirror and lost his last thread of control.

He threw his head back and howled, not a hunting howl or a calling howl but one of sheer, desolate misery.

While he was drawing breath for a second bout of howls, the men's room door opened and little claws skittered across the tile floor. Audacity rushed to him mewing nonstop and, without waiting for permission, started to climb him like a tiny mountaineer.

"She's terribly concerned, your daughter," Captain Valbuena stepped inside and closed the door. "Your squad mates are, as well. Alex, please, what's hurt you so badly?"

Wolf scooped Audacity into his arms to let her rub faces with him and pat him. For an embarrassingly long moment, all he could do was shake his head in answer while his breaths hitched and hiccupped.

"Alex…" The spare whisper was full of worry as the captain laid a hand on Wolf's shoulder.

He turned into that hand instinctively, seeking something besides misery and the captain folded both him and Audacity in his arms.

"Take a moment. As long as you need. Just know you're not alone."

Since he hadn't managed to make a complete idiot of himself yet, Wolf burst into tears and sobbed on Captain Valbuena's shoulder, choking out in fits and starts a short version of the previous night's conversation. He ignored the door opening and Kyle's soft 'everything Okay?' as Wolf poured out things he would normally find too private.

When he ran out of words and sobs, Captain Valbuena patted his chest and set him back. He limped in front of the stalls, lips pursed. "I've done a terrible thing, haven't I?"

"Sir?" Wolf shifted Audacity to the crook of one arm so he could wipe his eyes while she purred like a tiny motorboat against him.

"Could I confess something to you?"

"What? Sir."

Jeff poked his head in. "Oh. Sorry, sorry. Everything under control, sir?" He ducked out when Valbuena nodded.

The captain leaned against the wall, arms crossed. "I wanted to steal you from him. From Jason. I actually had some of the same thoughts he had. That he wasn't enough for you, a mere human. That he couldn't possibly be what you needed."

"Oh, um…"

"But I've watched you together. Seen how you look at him. How all of you *yearns* toward him when he's in the room. And I'm sorry. I was wrong and I've made a terrible mess here."

"Sir, no. It's not...I mean it *was* nice to dance with you."

Captain Valbuena laughed, though it sounded like it hurt. "You're too kind, my dear Officer Wolf."

Wolf's brain jumbled and stuck on what he'd been turning over and over all night. "I'm... It's like he wants me to...like he's saying I *should* have someone better."

Greg opened the door. "Oh. Sorry, sir. I'll, ah, just—" He backed out without finishing.

"Alex, you do know that sometimes humans and, incidentally, vampires, date more than one person at a time? So, for instance, I could be seeing you and Jeff simultaneously. That at times it works as long as everyone is honest?"

Wolf heaved a shaky sigh. "I guess for some people. It'd be okay. I just...it's not..."

"But it's not you," Captain Valbuena finished. "You are a one-man wolf. Your Jason has been feeling ordinary and inadequate next to you and I've only made the feeling worse."

"But I don't think he's ordinary!"

"And this is the conversation you should have with him rather than getting upset with him for seemingly pushing you away."

Vikash strode into the room, stopped and murmured, 'terribly sorry,' before he strode back out.

"Though in your defense," the captain went on as if he hadn't been interrupted again. "He picked the worst possible time for the conversation."

Audacity batted his nose. *Mew.*

"Okay. Maybe it wasn't what I thought. Maybe. Still. I know. I have to talk to him about it. Instead of howling." Wolf scratched his cub under her chin, calmer. Not happy but calmer. "Sir? You're not really going to ask Jeff out, are you?"

"Ah, no." Now the captain smiled. "I need lovers with a bit more heft to them. Nice man, but not my type—"

The door flew open with a crash. "Wolf? You need help in here?" Amanda stood on the threshold with Edgar on her shoulder.

"We're nearly done, Officer Zacchini." The captain's tone was chill and forbidding.

"Good, 'cause you've got a squad room full of worried people out here who're taking turns trying to sneak over here and make sure Wolf's okay. And the sneak parade's getting really annoying. Sir."

"Crapper hogger!" Edgar croaked, combing his neon pink beak through Amanda's dark hair.

"Ah. My apologies." Captain Valbuena offered a little bow. "Officer Wolf, if you're feeling able to face the world?"

"Yes, sir. I'm okay." Wolf sidled past Amanda on his way out, Audacity batting at Edgar's tail. "Sorry, Manda."

"S'okay, big guy. Was just starting to wonder if the captain had eaten you or you'd eaten him."

"Vamp sashimi!" Edgar called as he fluffed up his feathers.

"You realize you're very lucky that I don't enjoy fowl," Captain Valbuena muttered.

Audacity's head whipped around so she could hurl a fierce kitten hiss at the captain, who held up both hands in surrender.

"Little miss, I will never devour anyone under your protection. I swear on my very bones."

She settled back in Wolf's arms with a little growl-huff as if to say, *Well, yeah, you better remember it.*

"And I thought we were friends now." The captain tilted his head to address Audacity.

Miw. Mre-eh.

"Pretty sure she says you are, sir, but you better watch your step," Amanda supplied.

Back in the squad room, Krisk raised a brow ridge at Wolf and rolled a hand in an obvious question.

"I'm okay. Better, anyway." Wolf buried his face against Audacity's soft fur once more before he set her down. "I just haven't had a good humaning morning."

Krisk nodded while he typed on his phone.

Contact Jason.

"Yeah, was just about to." Wolf sent Jason a quick text about grabbing lunch at Morgan's Pier and Jason agreed with a little heart sticker thing. *That has to be good, doesn't it?*

Sure, Morgan's was a beer garden but with a beautiful October day, Wolf wanted to be outside. The food was good, with Krisk-friendly things on the menu. They had a bunch of different kinds of tables, with plenty of both sun and shade depending on who wanted what.

They arrived a few minutes late due to a 'dragon' call—an escaped monitor lizard—and found Jason and his partner Julie waiting for them out front.

She took Krisk by the arm and led him through the entrance arch, saying, "Let's give these two a little space, Officer Krisk, and we'll talk about frogs."

"Don't put Krisk to sleep with amphibian research, Jules." Jason rolled his eyes.

"Krisk likes to talk about my research. Unlike certain boring people I work with." Julie turned her head to stick her tongue out while Krisk let his tail down with a mighty thud that cut off further bickering.

They made their way to a table in the shade while Jason and Wolf headed for one in the center where the sun shone. Jason ordered the roast beef sandwich and Wolf tried to convince his stomach that it was hungry enough for a burger. He hoped the queasiness would die down once they started talking.

"Hey." Jason reached across to grip his arm. "You haven't told me what happened the other night. With the ceramic animals."

That's what Jason wants to start with? Easing into it, maybe. "We, um, found where they come from but it didn't go so well."

"Right. We did get that far."

"Oh. Yeah." Wolf sipped at his water, staring out over the river. "The woman who made the ceramic ones? She didn't believe us about the full-sized doubles. Didn't believe what she made could be dangerous. Captain wanted to confiscate the ceramics and her book. She got mad and tossed us out."

"She picked you up? The three of you?"

"Not with her hands." Wolf shook his head and stopped to thank the waitress who brought their food. "With her mind. Her magic. Then she tossed the captain a second time."

"Christ," Jason breathed out. "So she poses a threat to the city? Did she do the dust bunnies, too?"

Wolf took a bite to consider his answer. The burger was good. Juicy. Maybe he *was* hungry. "Pecca's not... She doesn't mean to be dangerous. She's alone and, what's the word? Naïve? Her other animals don't make doubles. Carr calls the ceramic ones, um…" Wolf had to consult the notes on his phone. "A life-casting *tsukumogami*."

"A…what?"

"An object that gets animated, the *tsukumogami*, but different 'cause these make living copies of themselves. Maybe they control the copies. We're not sure."

Jason chewed slowly, absorbing. "How does all that make this woman, Pecca, *not* dangerous?"

"It's the book." Wolf walked back through the conversations. Had he mentioned it? Jason's eyebrows drawing together said no. "A man in black, and yeah, we think it's the same one from the other times. He gave her a book with hoax animal paintings. Beautiful book. But it's what she uses to make the ceramics and bring them to life. Said she couldn't do it with ceramics before."

"Got it. So you're thinking this evil bastard's taking advantage of someone powerful but really sheltered."

"Yeah."

"So powerful she could toss an old vamp, twice, and break his hip."

Wolf blew out a slow breath. "Defending her home and her friends. She was really nice until the captain threatened her animals."

"Captain Richard couldn't charm her, huh?" Jason asked, a wary light in his eyes.

"Could've been more patient with her, yeah." Wolf polished off his burger, the fries left abandoned as he came around to what he needed to talk about. "Jason… The thing… What you said that night."

"I think I said a couple things that should've waited. Which thing?"

"The, um…" Wolf felt ridiculous but dropped his voice to a whisper. "Not being enough thing."

Jason mouth twisted in a grimace. He started to reach for Wolf's hand, then stopped himself and sat back. "I'm so, so sorry. I don't think I could've done it any more wrong—"

Wolf surged up as the scent hit him. Fired ceramic. In a crowd at lunchtime. If he was picking it up despite all the food scents, he was probably already too late.

"Krisk!" he called out as he cast about desperately for anything out of place.

An unholy shriek split the air above Krisk's table. He and Julie were already out of their chairs reacting to Wolf's shout. As Krisk turned toward the inhuman cry, a gray shape dropped out of the tree, snarling and spitting. It was… *Dear mother of gods.*

"Julie! Snag the grab nets and the tranq!" Jason's voice was close behind Wolf as he vaulted tables to reach Krisk in time as screaming patrons scattered out of his way.

The thing attacking him had eight-inch curved claws and sabretooth fangs. Krisk held it at arm's length while it slashed through his sleeves and twisted for a better angle. The body shape was round and ungainly for a predator, though the tufted ears were teddy bear cute. If it had been a little smaller without the oversized killing tools, it might have been a—

"Koala?" Wolf yelled over its shrieking.

"Drop bear!" Jason called back. "Don't get in the way of those claws!"

Wolf circled, trying to see if there was a good way to grab hold. "It's a *real* animal?"

"No, just a hoax animal I recognize."

Krisk shot him a look that clearly said, *It's real enough, thanks.* His grip slipped just as Julie raced back in with the equipment. The drop bear got a good slash at his chest, lines of shocking red against Krisk's gray-green skin. Most of the lunch crowd had fled the beer garden's courtyard in the domino effect of people running and screaming, though one young man who had been getting the action on his phone fainted.

"Krisk, we're gonna get him netted but you'll have to yank your hands free of the frame, okay? You and Wolf concentrate on getting civilians out if it gets away from us." Jason stood behind the drop bear with Julie, both of them on opposite sides of the hinged grab net.

Julie did a quick three count. They lunged, snagging the snarling monster and wrestling the frame closed as Krisk snatched his hands back. He stood panting, eyes too wide, while Wolf added his weight to the net and Julie shot a tranquilizer into the drop bear. It would take time to work, so none of them eased off the net as their catch thrashed and roared.

"Where's the second one? There's always two, right?" Jason grunted and hissed as a claw caught his hand through the net.

"Don't see it yet." Wolf leaned harder, trying to keep the drop bear better confined. "May be hiding."

While the three of them had their hands full, a hint of movement caught the corner of Wolf's eye. He turned his head just in time to see a second drop bear leap from the tree onto Krisk's back. Snorting and scrabbling behind him, Krisk twisted as he tried to dislodge it but it clung tight. Even when he flung himself on his back, the drop bear hung on by digging its claws between his collarbones and biting deep into his shoulder.

Wolf's attention swiveled between the drop bear trying to kill his boyfriend and the one trying to kill his partner. "I've had enough of this."

He pulled his arm back and punched the netted drop bear in the face, which earned him cut knuckles, but it settled down. That done, he hurled himself across the intervening space to Krisk, flipped him onto his front and grabbed the second drop bear by its scruff to get it to let go with its teeth so Wolf could yank it off his partner.

It snarled and snapped, doing its best to fasten onto the new threat. Wolf slammed it against the pavement to stun it while Jason hurried up with the second grab net. Jaw tight, avoiding Wolf's eyes, he got a tranquilizer dart into the drop bear while it was still.

"I'm sorry," Wolf murmured. "I know that wasn't right."

"Can't say much. Really can't," Jason said as he shook his head. "You had to save Krisk."

Wolf made the *officer down* call as he tried to assess where the bleeding was worst. The wounds at Krisk's shoulders were deep and ugly and Krisk himself was terribly still. Julie's drop bear was sleeping now or unconscious from being punched, so she ran for the first aid kit from the truck, then helped Wolf put pressure on the bleeding slashes. Krisk's ribcage still rose and fell. He still had a heartbeat but he was terribly cold.

"Hang on, old friend," Wolf whispered to him. He wanted to make some joke about the department never being able to find another suitable partner for him when the nearby scent of a ceramic animal distracted him.

There. Both of the ceramic drop bears lurked under a nearby table. Growling low in his throat, Wolf lunged. Chairs flew, two tables crashed over, but he had the little bastards this time. He pounced as they tried to flee, caught one in his left hand and the other under his knee. A terrible crunch made him wince. He lifted his knee to find the second miniature drop bear shattered in a hundred glittering shards.

He didn't even have time to regret the destruction before a loud *pop* came from behind him. Wolf whipped around, certain someone was shooting, but everyone was staring in shock at the second grab net. The now *empty* grab net that had just snapped shut.

"Where is it?" Wolf demanded as he corralled the remaining miniature with both hands.

"It just *poof*. Vanished," Julie said with a squeak.

The ceramic had to exist before the life-sized animal. When the ceramic was destroyed— "Um, I think I killed it."

"You what now?" Jason stopped poking at the empty net.

"I smashed the little ceramic guy and the live one popped out of being. Can we…? Jason, do you have a bag for this other one? It keeps stabbing my palms."

"Jesus, Mary and Joseph," Julie huffed out. "What the *hell* have you boys gotten into now?"

Jason produced a reptile bag from his belt pouch and helped Wolf pop his captured ceramic inside. "I'll explain everything later, Jules." Jason hissed as he glanced at Wolf's palms. "You going with Krisk? Someone should look at those."

Twin sirens wailed up the street, ambulance and squad car. Wolf nodded and fished his keys out. "Ask someone to drive our car back to the station. I'd go with Krisk anyway."

"Okay." Jason grabbed him by the back of the neck and shook gently. "Gonna be all right, babe?"

"I'm…" *Exhausted. Numb. Worried sick. Trying to put things in order.* "Thinking. I'll be okay. Glad you were here."

Jason leaned in for a quick kiss. "I'll call you when we get everything squared away. No. Never mind. I'll meet you at the hospital. You'll need a ride anyway, right?"

"Yeah. Okay." Wolf made his way over to Krisk and plunked down near him, not so close that he'd be in the way of the paramedics. "Okay."

Just gonna sit here by Krisk, make sure he keeps breathing and try to figure out what all this stuff I know now should mean.

Chapter Eleven

The squad car screaming up the street had been Kyle's, who had both of the rookies with him that day. Jason couldn't remember their names but he was impressed at how good Kyle was as a field instructor, getting them to bag up the remains of the smashed ceramic drop bear, having one phone Dr. Moreau so she could get down to the ER and ordering the other out front to corral witnesses.

"What's the official line, Eva?" Kyle asked before the woman rookie went out front.

"Wild cat attack. All under control."

Kyle clapped her on the shoulder with a bright smile. "You got it. I'll be out in a sec to help." His smile fell when he turned to Jason. "How bad is it?"

"Looks bad. Krisk lost a lot of blood. I just don't know enough about his physiology to make any guesses. Alex's hands are sliced up and I think he's shocky. Glassy-eyed. Shivering. Didn't even give me an argument about going in the ambulance."

Kyle let out a low whistle. "Good he's going, then. You guys all right?"

"Yeah. Me and Jules got off easy. Your intrepid officers did all the hard stuff." Jason held the keys out. "Alex asked if someone could take his car back."

"I'll have one of my minions do it." Kyle bounced Alex's keys on his palm. "Could you do me a favor? Could you hold on to the, ah, drop bears? I need to be sure we have a place to safely hold them until State decides to send someone. Since we already have other entities in holding."

"Woofen-poofs and tripoderos."

"Now, see, I was trying not to say those ridiculous words. They promised me that being a police officer did not include ridiculous words."

Jason managed a strained chuckle. "No problem. The truck's about as secure as it gets and the weather's good so it won't get too hot in there for the biological drop bear. And that's not a phrase I ever thought I'd say."

"Thanks, Jason. Better go see how Eva's doing." Kyle squinted at him a moment. "Puppies and kittens. Of course. What else would it be?"

He left Jason gaping after him. Under other circumstances, he might've asked what Kyle meant, but there was too much to do. The paramedics hurried Krisk and Alex away as quickly as they could, then Jason concentrated on getting equipment cleaned up and stowed and the tranquilized drop bear documented. Weight, length, vitals—even for a hoax animal, they still had to do the charts. Finally, they secured it, since it seemed to be without gender, in one of the large dog cages and got its ceramic counterpart closed up in the mostly empty metal first aid kit. He took the truck to the hospital so he would be closer to the 77th when Kyle let him know about drop bear housing and Julie hitched a ride with Kyle, who dropped her at their office.

By the time he reached the ER, they'd already transferred Krisk up to an isolation room so Dr. Moreau would have space to work. He found Alex sitting in one of the big armchairs by the bed, holding Krisk's clawed hand in his bandaged one.

"Hey." Jason pulled up one of the smaller plastic chairs. "How's he doing?"

Wolf shook his head, drew a shaky breath then buried his head against Jason's shoulder. Jason wrapped both arms around him, rubbing both hands up and down, waiting for Alex to catch himself.

"He's…" Alex heaved another shuddering breath. "Dr. Moreau says it's too early and that she doesn't know enough to predict. He's kinda…hibernating. She called it his power save mode."

"Okay. I know it doesn't look good." It didn't. Krisk was that terrible dusty gray some lizards turned near death. "But he's strong. He's stubborn. And since he has a hibernation mode, we know he's fighting."

"Yeah." Alex nuzzled against him and Jason knew better than to think it was anything but seeking comfort from his scent. A few minutes of quiet snuffling ended with, "What happened to the drop bear I didn't murder?"

Jason kissed the top of his head and squeezed him tight. "We don't even know if the hoax animals are properly alive. I mean, they don't even exist without the ceramic creations."

"I murdered the ceramic one."

"It was an accident. Are you going to tell me it's all your fault Krisk got hurt?"

"It was my idea to go to Morgan's."

"Hey. Knock it off. You saved lots of people, which is what you do, and I don't think it matters where we were. You guys have stalkers." Jason waited for Alex to nod against him. "Anyway. Drop bear's asleep in the truck outside. Both versions."

Again Alex nodded but he'd tensed, toying with a button on Jason's shirt.

"What?" Jason asked softly. "What did you think of?"

Alex surged up, though he didn't let go of Jason or Krisk's hand. "We need to go see her."

"Her, who?" Jason's tired brain turned the last few days over. "Pecca?"

"Yeah. We need to go see her. Now. With the drop bear in the truck. I need to talk to her."

"Sounds like she doesn't want to talk to anyone."

Alex stood and nuzzled at the side of Krisk's face. "I have to try. Jason?"

For you? Anything. "Of course. Now, or wait until it's dark since that's when you visited before?"

"Now. Not wasting another second. Don't want anyone else hurt."

I don't want you hurt. "Let's go."

* * * *

"Um, babe? How do you even know where the house is?" Jason's eyebrows had crept together in a dubious frown.

In the daytime, the end of the street looked like it was supposed to according to internet images. Railroad tracks, a little bit of pavement and a decrepit, cobbled-together fence just beyond. Nothing else. No cute, well-kept house and garden. But Wolf could smell it. The kiln, the old wood scent of the floors, the herbs growing in Pecca's garden, Pecca herself — it was all there.

"She can hide it, but I don't think she can move it."

"Oh." Jason squinted at the apparently empty lot in front of them. "Just so you know, not reassured."

Wolf squeezed his shoulder. "She might just ignore me. Guess we'll see." He pulled in a deep breath and bellowed, "Pecca! Pecca Teecosi, it's Officer Wolf! I need to talk to you!"

A breeze blew a ripped paper bag across the pavement. A cricket chirped its cool-weather cadence. No Pecca, no house appearing.

"Ms. Pecca! The vampire's not with me, promise. I have one of your drop bears out here."

A minute went by, then two. Wolf heaved a sigh, about to tell Jason thanks for going along with his stupid plan when a door appeared in midair. He squinted hard, just about able to make out the lines of the house.

Pecca stuck her head out. "You might be lying, Officer Wolf. Who's that with you? He looks angry."

"This is Jason Shen. He works for animal control and he's a very nice human. That's his *I'm not sure about all this* face." Wolf pointed to the truck. "He helped us catch the drop bear. Please, Ms. Pecca. At least come out and see. There's... I want to tell you what's happened."

She tipped her head left and right, regarding him as if she were a songbird. "I'm coming out. But only because you sound so upset."

"*That's* your powerful witch?" Jason leaned close to whisper. "Looks more like a Carol Kane character if Carol were younger, biracial and taller."

The door vanished behind Pecca when she closed it. She hurried down the invisible steps and joined them at the truck. A line between her eyes betrayed worry. Bloodshot eyes said she'd had a terrible night. "Show me."

"We had the drop bear sedated, ma'am." Jason unlocked the truck's back door and hesitated. "But it's probably waking up by now. Please be careful."

She gave Jason an odd look, then stepped up to the truck to peer inside at the cage Jason indicated. The drop bear's eyes were open, glittering in the dim light inside the truck. It snarled and lunged, oversized fangs snapping as Pecca leaned closer to investigate. Without flinching, she frowned and bent to examine its claws.

"He's very fierce. But maybe he's just a random drop bear."

Wolf stared at her with his mouth open. Of all the things she might have said, he hadn't expected that. Something about the way she said it, though, as she shifted from foot to foot, her scent suddenly nervous.

"Um... I guess." Wolf reached over to unlatch the first aid kit. "I guess we thought that, too. When we saw the jackalopes. But every time. Every time we've come across the hoax animals, your beautiful ceramic ones have been right there, too."

He opened the box to show her the surviving drop bear figurine and her frown deepened.

"Why's there only one?"

"I... Ms. Pecca, I smashed the other one. Trying to catch them both. Didn't want to, but I landed on it. I'm sorry."

She turned to him and put a hand flat on his chest. It was hard not to drop his gaze, her eyes were so sad.

"Officer Who Was Once a Wolf, you're very honest. I'm not happy, but thank you for not fibbing." Pecca turned to frown at the drop bear again, holding one hand out near the large drop bear and the other over the figurine. "They vibrate the same. Echoes of each other. All of my ceramics are making blood and bone copies?"

Strange way to put it. "All of the ones we've seen, yes, ma'am."

Jason spoke up softly, as if he was afraid to startle her. "They've done some real harm, Ms. Teecosi. This last attack was the worst."

"How silly." She flapped a hand at Jason. "All of my critters are peaceful. They'd never hurt anyone."

"Do you remember Officer Lizard Person?" Wolf asked.

"Oh, yes. He was very nice."

"Come with me to visit him, please. In the hospital."

She scrunched her nose. "I don't like hospitals."

"I don't know anyone who does." Jason jerked his head toward the truck, obviously picking up on what Wolf intended. "Just come with us to see him. We won't stay long."

"I'll be right back."

Pecca ran up the invisible steps, her skirts flying, and her house blinked into sight when she went inside, only to vanish again when the door shut. She returned clutching a folded blanket knitted out of sparkly blue and green yarn.

"Present," she explained as she hopped up onto the truck's bench seat. "You shouldn't go visiting at the hospital without a present."

Pecca was more her animated self during the drive, chatting about how she seldom rode in cars, but buses were nice and how the city looked different from a car, though she didn't go out often. She grew quiet as they reached the hospital, though.

Wolf watched as she withdrew into herself, clutching his hand as he led her inside, and he wondered if this was too cruel. It hurt him to cause her distress but she kept saying that her animals would never harm anyone. If they were going to stop the rampaging hoax animals from doing worse things than they already had, though? She had to accept they were dangerous first.

Jason kept her talking on the way up to Krisk's room—about knitting, about the neighborhood where she lived, about tea and herb gardens—his easy, comfortable style of conversation far better at putting people at ease. Pecca's shaking telegraphed to Wolf but she held up well until they reached Krisk's room. She took one look at the bed, buried her face against Wolf's chest and burst into tears.

"Poor Officer Lizard," she wailed. "He's dead!"

Wolf shot a quick glance at the monitor readouts. He didn't know what the numbers *meant* for Krisk but there were still numbers. "No, Ms. Pecca. He's not."

"Come see him." Jason held out both hands. "I think he knows we're here."

In hesitant steps, she joined Jason by the bedside, sheltering in the circle of his arms. She held a hand over Krisk's chest with her eyes squeezed shut. "No. He's so cold but he's still connected. What happened to Officer Lizard?"

"There were two drop bears hiding in a beer garden today. The first one he held off so that no one else would be hurt. The second ambushed him shamefully," Jason explained gently. "Their teeth and claws are deadly and they're scary aggressive. If it'd been someone smaller, someone not as brave and strong as Officer Krisk, it's pretty clear they wouldn't have survived."

Tears still tracked down Pecca's face. "And my critters were there?"

"They were. Right there."

Pecca sniffled. "There were...other times?"

"The tripoderos attacked a crowd of people who were there to help animals. No one was critically hurt but a vampire suffered sunstroke trying to catch one and Officer Wolf was badly bruised. The woofen-poofs attacked a group of small children. Again, no one was hurt, but only because Officer Wolf reacted so quickly. The jackalopes attacked people in the park. One of them was me." Jason tugged his shirt up to show her the antler punctures in his side.

Carefully, she spread her blanket present over Krisk's feet, away from all the wires and tubes. Then she sat on the end of the bed, petting his ankle and sobbing quietly.

"Mama said," she whispered. "Mama said never to do harm. It was the most important thing. The thing at the center of things. And I have. I didn't meant to, like Officer Wolf didn't mean to squash the drop bear. But I have."

"We can fix it." Jason went to one knee beside her and took her hands in his. "Someone has *used* you to do harm. He somehow knew what would draw you in and he misled you. You didn't want any of this. We'll help you. Whatever you need to fix this."

She stared at him long and hard, chewing on her lower lip. "You're a nice man, Mr. Shen. I think the animals all like you, don't they?"

"A lot of them do."

Wolf held his breath, in awe of Jason's ability to calm and soothe, to connect. It was like watching a master bridge builder, though Jason built word bridges. He didn't stumble into the river as Wolf would have, caught in undercurrents and eddies of confusion. No, he had an instinct for the distance across and he reached. If anyone could reach Pecca, strange as she was, he could.

"We have to fix this," she repeated his words in a whisper. She stood slowly, still holding on to Jason, moving their joined hands up and down. "We have to *fix* this."

"Back to the house?" Jason suggested.

She nodded and after one final pat to Krisk's foot, she scampered out of the room, hauling Jason behind her. Wolf blinked in shock, scrambled to catch up and managed to make the elevator with them before the door closed in his face.

On the drive back, Pecca insisted on sitting next to the window. Not the best thing with Wolf squashed in the middle with a steadying hand on the headliner so he wouldn't smack into Jason around turns, but she soon showed she had a reason. Now that she knew her ceramic creations were routinely slipping off her property, she had to call them back. She let out the sharp whistles that called her handmade critters to her all the way back to the house. Jason had barely thrown the truck into park when she leaped out and raced for the house, forcing them to hurry after her.

Pecca was still whistling through her teeth, three sharp notes separated by a half tone. When Wolf and Jason caught up to her in the kitchen, she'd retrieved the big red book of hoax animals and stood by the table, whistling and whistling. Ceramic animals began to arrive in scurries, hops, flaps and waddles. They congregated around her feet and she began to lift them to the counter, naming them as she placed them.

"Jackalopes, hodags, tripoderos, woofen-poofs, fatulivas, hoopsnakes, miniature water buffalo…" She ran out of animals and glanced around on the floor, lifting chairs, checking under the table. "Where are the snipes?"

After several searches of the floor, she finally glanced up and managed a watery smile. "There you are." From behind the flour canister, she lifted two odd little birds with long, ungainly legs and beaks shaped vaguely like sporks. "They're really shy. I'll…need the little drop bear."

"Ms. Pecca? What are you going to do?"

"I have to…to end this." She waved a hand at her dutifully lined up critters and included the book in the sweep. "All of this."

"Wait. Please." Wolf stepped forward to put himself between her and the book. "I need to call the captain. Can we wait until I know if it's okay?"

"Captain Vampire?" She shrugged. "I don't know what he has to do with it, but all right."

Wolf fumbled pulling up his contacts and putting the call through, afraid she would change her mind. When Captain Valbuena answered, his voice was sharp and testy, "Officer Wolf? Where in all the mother's teats *are* you?"

"Sir?"

"You were supposed to be at the hospital but apparently you simply wandered off."

"Yes, sir. Sorry about that. Things, um, came up." Wolf pulled in a breath and hurried on, not waiting for more of the reprimand. "Sir, we're with Pecca Teecosi. ACO Shen and I. At her house."

"How the *devil* did you manage that? Wait, you're not being forcibly held, are you?"

"No, sir. Ms. Teecosi, though, she's seen what her ceramics do and she wants to, ah, take care of things."

"She's going to destroy the book? No, no, tell her she can't. That book needs to be in custody." Captain Valbuena hissed through his teeth. "I'm coming down there."

"Sir, I'm not sure that's a good idea. She, um, I don't think Ms. Teecosi likes you."

"Since when does *like* have anything to do with it?"

Wolf stared up at the ceiling, certain he was crossing a line. "How's your hip, sir?"

A low growl came through loud and clear. "Are you being smart with me?"

"No, sir. Just making a point."

"Damn it, Alex." Captain Valbuena huffed, most likely pacing. "I'm coming down there. Don't endanger yourself, but try to preserve that book."

Wolf disconnected and turned to Pecca. "You probably heard him. He wants the book saved."

"What would he do with the book?" she asked.

"He'd take it up to State Paranormal Police HQ. Magic experts would study it. Try to find out where it came from. Maybe who gave it to you."

Pecca's eyes narrowed. "Officer Wolf. Can you tell me there are no bad people there?"

What? "I…"

"Experts. Probably powerful mages and stuff. Can you tell me there aren't any bad ones? Who might use the book for other things?"

"I don't...know. I don't know everyone there." Wolf foundered, losing words faster than he could find them. "It's...safe. I mean, they're careful. Safeguards."

Pecca nodded. "That's what I thought. You don't know, though you're honest and said so." She leaned back against her stove, gaze sweeping across her animals. "I'd like to save the snipes. They'd never hurt anything. The miniature buffalo, too. The real life ones would be no more than five inches high."

"Tell us what to do, Ms. Pecca. Your house, your book," Jason said. "It has to be your decision what happens here."

Wolf wanted to disagree. He wanted to say, no, he was obligated to retrieve that book. But regulations were a little cloudy on some issues. If an object or creature posed a clear and present danger, onsite destruction was at the discretion of the officer in the field. Besides, the captain hadn't *ordered* him to save the book. He'd said to try. He'd tried, so now he kept his mouth shut.

"Mr. Shen, if you could take the buffalo and the snipes out to your truck. And..." Pecca swallowed hard. "And bring me the drop bear."

Jason tucked the selected animals into his shirt pockets and hurried out of the kitchen.

"Leave the front door open!" Pecca called after him.

Her eyes swam with tears again and Wolf couldn't blame her. She was about to kill her own creations. Murdering her friends. What a horrible thought. When Jason returned, holding the ceramic drop bear by its back so it couldn't stab him, Pecca took the critter from him and whistled to it as she placed it on the counter with the rest. The lone drop bear sat quietly beside the tripoderos. The entire line of ceramic creatures gave off an air of waiting.

"Ms. Pecca?" Wolf murmured.

"Stay behind me." Her dark brown eyes had taken on a silvery glow. "You're both very nice. I don't want you to get hurt."

She planted her feet at the head of the table so she faced both the book and the lineup of her creations. A light indoor breeze began, tugging at Wolf's hair. Pecca pointed a finger near the stand mixer and her pipe cleaner elephant floated out from behind the bowl. She transported him gently into the hallway.

"*Chiudi la porta*," she whispered and a red glow veiled the kitchen doorway. "So none of the other little ones can come in."

The wind rose. Wolf grabbed Jason into a bear hug and took another step back. He had a bad feeling things were going to get messy. Jason had a good hold on Wolf's shirtfront, wary and watchful, and Wolf knew him well enough to be sure he wasn't clinging. He was preparing to throw them both to the floor if things started flying.

"I'm sorry, babies. It's not your fault," Pecca whispered. "I'm so sorry."

The book thumped open on the table, pages riffling in the wind. Pecca raised both hands, her bell sleeves snapping, her skirts whipping around her legs.

"*Separare! Distruggere!*"

A page ripped from the book, lifted in a mini-cyclone above the table and burst into vivid orange flames. Amidst its crackling came the ripping of more pages. Pecca's hair twisted about her head in reaching-anemone arms of auburn. Page after page burst into flame.

Wolf slapped a hand on the wall to steady them as the floor lurched, a sole-shaking growl rumbling through the linoleum. He squinted against the sting as ash joined the swirling winds. The animals on the counter shifted and bumped against each other in restless shuffling. The tripoderos raised their snouts. The woofen-poofs flapped and shrieked. The surviving drop bear crouched low, gathering itself.

"Pecca, look out!" Wolf yelled as the ceramic drop bear launched itself in an impossible leap toward Pecca's face.

Pecca shot a hand out toward it and shouted, "*Ha!*" the single syllable echoing and huge in the confined space, rendering Wolf momentarily deaf.

The drop bear shattered into pottery dust in midair, tiny shining particles joining the tornado. Pecca accelerated the page tearing, one beautiful watercolor after another devoured in ravenous flames. The woofen-poofs launched at Pecca just as the hodags with their rows of sharp teeth leaped from the counter. She ducked the woofen-poofs without breaking her chanting, fending them off with one arm as they dove for her eyes.

She won't be able to fight off all of them. Wolf shoved Jason to the floor and lunged for the hodags. He let the pair of them latch on to his bandaged hands. Blood and ceramic chips flew as he slammed them against the floor. Pecca ripped out the woofen-poofs page and destroyed it with a sudden fireball. They cracked and crumbled mid-air, falling as nothing but powder.

The damaged book shook and rattled on the table. Jagged green bolts shot from it in all directions, melting wallpaper, burning holes through furniture. Pecca threw up a protective wall of light in front of her, never losing the rhythm of her chanting and thank every god that Jason was behind that wall. But the book wasn't done.

It shimmered and shook hard enough that the table legs skittered on the floor as one by one the life-sized versions of the remaining hoax animals teleported into the kitchen. Despite having been locked away in holding at the station, the jackalopes, tripoderos and hoopsnakes were among them.

The tripoderos immediately began firing, the trajectory of their dirt-pellet missiles erratic and more dangerous in the swirling magic wind. The hoopsnakes rushed Wolf and knocked him to the floor before he could regain his feet. The jackalopes charged Pecca's protective wall, their antlers tearing through as they went after Jason. The fatu liva birds, sleek and streamlined with sharp, hooked beaks, took to the air and dropped hard, cube-shaped objects indiscriminately. One of those broke open on Wolf's shoulder with a painful crack and he realized the acidic innards burning his skin were the yolk and white of eggs.

Wolf tried to grab hold of the snakes but his hands were bloody and slippery on their scales. He couldn't fight free of them. As soon as he thought he had one, the second one knocked him over.

Kitchen chair in one hand, metal serving tray held over his head with the other, Jason held back the charging jackalopes and kept the cube eggs off his head as he backed up on his knees through the hole in Pecca's protective wall.

"Jason, wait!"

Wolf held a hoopsnake down with his knee and managed to get the other behind the head just as one of the jackalopes decided he was a better target. It charged him and speared his arm, pinning them both to a table leg. Frantic to reach Jason, Wolf took the weaponized hare by its scruff and tried to yank them loose, but the angle was bad and the snakes kept smacking into him.

He could only watch in horror as Jason left Pecca's protection and leaned into the maelstrom, making his slow way toward the counter. The fatu livas and tripoderos concentrated their attacks on him, the metal tray soon dented and pitted by the overwhelming barrage. Jason, stubborn and steady, persisted in his slow-motion charge.

When he reached the counter, he stood, trying his best to shield himself with the tray. He gained his feet and dropped the tray, its clang muffled by the roaring winds and shrieks of angry birds, who redoubled their efforts to bring him down. Jason gripped the chair in both hands, lifted it with a frustrated roar, and brought it down hard on the herd of ceramic animals still on the counter. Ceramic flew from broken figurines and canisters, his swings indiscriminate and thoroughly destructive.

One by one, the flesh and blood copies winked out of existence—no more fatu livas swooping, no more hoopsnakes tormenting Wolf. He fell forward when the jackalope pinning him to the table vanished. "Jason?"

"I'm okay," Jason croaked from somewhere across the kitchen. "I'm...yeah."

On the table, the book slammed shut, shuddered violently and burst into flames. Pecca made a few ineffective swipes at her wild hair and the winds died as she folded her arms, watching the book of evil intent burn.

"Shouldn't we get it off your table, Ms. Pecca?" Wolf asked as he cradled his arm against his chest.

"No. It's a magic fire. It's fine there." Pecca's eyes widened as she took in the state of her guests. "Mr. Shen, you'll want to run that hand under cold water." She nodded at Jason's hand where one of the fatu liva eggs had split open. "Officer Wolf...you poor thing."

She wasn't satisfied until Wolf had struggled out of his shirt and she'd re-bandaged his hand and seen to his antler-impaled arm. It wasn't until she'd finished and Jason had joined him at the table with ice on the back of his hand that Wolf became aware of his phone buzzing. He pulled it from his pocket delicately, careful of his wrapped hands, and read through the several, increasingly irate texts on his phone.

"Um. Captain's outside."

"Yes, I know," Pecca said, not looking up from sweeping the floor.

"He'd like to come in, please?"

She tapped her fingers on the broom handle. "He sounds angry again. Do you really want me to let him in?"

No, Wolf didn't really want her to, but not letting him in would only make him angrier. "Yes, please."

"All right. But he needs to behave this time." She whispered a few words and the room brightened a fraction, as if the sun had come out from behind a thin cloud cover.

A moment later the front door slammed open and Captain Valbuena's boots stomped through the hall. His jaw looked ready to break and red tinged his eyes. He wasn't angry. He was furious. The scene in the kitchen stopped him from bellowing immediately and his planned bellow probably wasn't what he ended up shouting.

"What the *hell* happened in here?"

"Magical firefight, sir."

"I see." Some of the fire drained from Captain Valbuena's eyes. "Everyone all right? Should I even ask what happened to the book?"

"Mostly, sir. Visit to Urgent Care's probably not a bad idea." Wolf swallowed against the ash and ceramic dust in his throat. "Book went up in flames, sir. It, ah, resisted arrest."

"It's gone, Captain Vampire. My beautiful book, my beautiful babies, they had to be put down." She attempted to straighten her hair again, though half of the tightly curled strands fell back in her face. "You were right. They were making angry real animals. And they hurt poor Officer Lizard. I couldn't tell myself it was a lie anymore."

"Ah." Captain Valbuena put a hand over his heart and gave her a little bow. "Shame about the book. But thank you for understanding the danger. I *am* sorry about your creatures. They were quite beautiful."

"Oh! The snipes and the miniature water buffalo," she cried out and rushed from the room.

Captain Valbuena raised an eyebrow. "The what?"

"We tried to save a couple of the harmless ceramics, Captain," Jason answered with a weary sigh. "I have the bad feeling we didn't manage."

Pecca returned with the open first aid kit from the truck. She managed a crooked smile even though a tear tracked down her cheek. "They're still pretty. I'll keep them, of course."

Tenderly, she placed the pair of snipe figurines on a clean counter spot and added the water buffalo pair.

They were inert, normal ceramic figures now, without a single crackle of magic between them.

She refused the captain's offer to help clean up her kitchen, though she did let him bag up some of the book ash in case the lab folks could puzzle anything out from it. Jason helped Wolf with a brief recounting of events, since Wolf kept hacking and coughing, and the captain nodded at the end of the report, seemingly satisfied.

"With the book itself on the attack, and I've no doubt it was controlling the creatures both biological and ceramic, I don't see that you had much choice. My report will reflect as much." He ushered Jason and Wolf ahead of him as they left, then hesitated in the doorway. "Ms. Pecca, do you ever animate existing objects? Say, for instance, a leather jacket or a green pea coat?"

Pecca shook her head, dislodging curls again. "No. That was more Mama's thing. She might have done a leather jacket once. I don't remember, though. Her animations sometimes just ran away and we wouldn't see them again."

The door shut. The house vanished behind them.

"So, do we tell LJ that we think we found his half-sister?" Jason asked as he stared at the deceptively empty lot.

"Maybe." Wolf coughed into the crook of his elbow. "Probably."

"Once upon a time," Captain Valbuena said wistfully, "I thought being a vampire police detective was as strange as the world got."

"Not anymore, sir?"

"Oh, not by a few hundred bizarre miles."

Chapter Twelve

The rens had arrived to retrieve Captain Valbuena and it gave Wolf a strange turn, watching them hug the captain fiercely in greeting as they shot murderous glances his way. Two men, two women, each fit and handsome in his or her own way and somehow evenly matched in height. Wolf was never going to think of Carrington as fussy again.

Captain Valbuena shook hands throughout the squad room, thanking everyone for their assistance, not even hesitating when he came to Carrington. He offered no apologies for earlier slights, but it was a step. Even LJ and Hunter received slightly awkward sleeve shakes and Edgar got an ironic salute toward where he lurked on his perch.

Finally, the captain came to where Wolf stood beside Lieutenant Dunfee. "Mia, I'll make the recommendations we talked about. I don't know if the brass will listen, but I'll do as I promised. You've good people here and certain biases from the top down shouldn't affect their careers so drastically."

"Thank you, Richard." She gave him a terse nod. "It was unexpectedly good to see you."

Captain Valbuena laughed at that and turned to take Wolf by the shoulders. "Alex, you were a goddess blessing. Thank you for looking after a stubborn, high-handed ass."

"Um, you're welcome, sir?"

"You're a good man, Alex." The captain gave him a solid clap on his arm. "Take good care of your Jason. Bravest animal control officer I've ever met."

"Yes, sir."

The rens helped the captain into his travel box, closed it securely and took him out to the transport van with practiced ease. The squad room seemed both emptier and lighter when they'd gone.

"Interesting vampire," Kash said from where he leaned against his desk.

Kyle shot him an incredulous look. "You liked him?"

"He grew on me."

"Ma'am?" Carrington called out from his corner. "Is it inappropriate to ask what he meant by recommendations?"

Lieutenant Dunfee stared out the window into the parking lot without a single twitch. Finally, she huffed. "It's not appropriate, no. But you knew that, Loveless. Captain Valbuena has several recommendations, only one of which I'll discuss. But you knuckleheads keep in mind that it's not his decision to make. He's recommending that we finally have access to detective track promotions here. The usual testing and process applies." She held up a hand to stop the several voices that tried to throw out questions. "Yes, even if you'd started on or completed the process prior to your transfer here. Paranormal division is different."

"Still, that's a big step in normalizing the department," Jeff said, though his smile was tentative.

"Also, Soren, you're back on the normal duty roster. I had the confirmation this afternoon."

Kyle jumped up and let out a whoop while Kash graced the lieutenant with that spare hint of a smile. "Thank you, ma'am. It'll be good to get back out there with Kyle."

"I didn't say you were returning to patrol with Monroe, did I?" Lieutenant Dunfee snapped and the squad froze, everyone anticipating the worst. "Married couples assigned together is frowned on in most departments. Monroe, you've been working well with Poole. Looks like you finally have someone you can work alongside and not cause a disaster."

"Um, thank you, ma'am?"

"Soren, you'll be partnered with Dennis. For the most part, I think you'll be a good influence. Just don't get ahead of yourself again." She turned from the window to face them. "Questions?"

"How's Krisk?" Amanda asked as she picked Audacity up from the floor.

Lieutenant Dunfee nodded to Wolf. He cleared his throat as everyone turned to him. "He's holding steady, Dr. Moreau says. She hates not being able to give him blood but, um, the hospital doesn't exactly have his blood type lying around. He's not as… Well… He looks better today. She says he should make it."

"Good. Squad room's not right without him."

All heads turned with nearly identical expressions of shock. That comment had come from Vance. He spread his hands. "What? What'd I say now?"

"You're good, Vance," Jeff patted his shoulder. "We just weren't expecting it."

"Krisk is cool," Vance muttered, slumping in his chair.

"Finish up for the day, ladies and gentlemen. Wolf, go home and take a couple of days. I saw you trying to type with those hands."

"Yes, ma'am." Face flushed with embarrassment, Wolf went to his desk to call his mom. Not only could he not type, he couldn't drive, either, and he felt like a kid at school having to wait for his parent to come pick him up.

LJ brought Audacity to him and retrieved her carrier from under the desk. He lingered, fidgeting with his sleeves, and Wolf thought that looked like a question.

"Are you going to see her? Pecca?"

With a sleeve wriggle, LJ indicated maybe. Or possibly a worm, but Wolf was leaning toward the *maybe*.

"Do you remember the house where you...? Um. Where you started being?"

LJ shrugged and flipped back through Wolf's desk calendar.

"Long time ago. Yeah. I don't remember much stuff from being a cub." Wolf petted Audacity with the non-bandaged tips of his fingers and she curled up purring in his lap. "Maybe you should take Hunter with you. You know, so you don't have to go alone."

One sleeve went up as if LJ were tapping his chin. Then he did his collar nod before drifting away, deep in jacket thought.

Mom came twenty minutes later, increasing the embarrassment since she insisted on coming inside to help him carry things rather than waiting for him to come out. What should've been a quick escape turned into another twenty minutes of Mom greeting everyone she knew and being introduced the new officers and knocking on the lieutenant's door to say hello since it would be rude not to. Wolf waited helplessly by his desk, knowing that nothing he could say would speed up matters by even a fraction of a second.

"At least your mother's friendly instead of predatory," Carrington offered on his way to the copier.

"And not super nosy," Kyle added from where he was going over routes with Jeremy.

"And she likes your boyfriend," Greg chimed in as he headed to the breakroom.

Jeff leaned back in his chair, 'porting a grape from one hand to the other. "She sends us all birthday cards, you know."

"I… No. Didn't know that." Wolf blinked. Though it shouldn't have surprised him. His mom did tend to adopt people.

Finally, Mom scooped Audacity into her carrier, grabbed both carrier and Wolf's lunch bag and whisked them away.

"Jason's still coming over, right?" Wolf asked as they got in the car. "You didn't tell him not to?"

Mom looked smug as she said, "Jason's already at the house making dinner."

"He's… You let him?"

Mom *tsked*. "He's not a bad cook. Just needs a little guiding on how to keep things neat and organized while he cooks."

"Huh."

"Have you and Jason talked?"

Wolf almost asked *about what*, but caught himself. He got it. Jason had been upset and had talked to Mom. Maybe that was a good thing? "We were trying to before some rude drop bears interrupted."

"I see. Well, I'm going out with Evonn and Carla this evening, so you boys go on and have dinner without me."

All set up. Nice and neat. Wolf just hoped the conversation went better this time.

* * * *

Miriam had planned it all so beautifully and had helped him with dinner, no matter what she said. Sure, Jason knew how to make a nice roast, one of his favorite things, but he wasn't always good about making sure there were other things to eat with the meat.

When Alex came through the door, he looked so tired, so done. Maybe better to put off any serious conversation? He could just feed his police officer and put him to bed... The unsaid things between them would probably keep Alex awake, though.

"All right, I'm going." Miriam put the carrier on the hall floor and unzipped the top so her desperately pawing granddaughter could jump out. "Be a good girl, Audi. Don't make a pest of yourself."

Miw. Audacity plopped down by her dad's shoe to make a show of primly washing her ears.

"Uh-huh. You're such an angel." Miriam stood on tiptoes to kiss Alex's cheek, then Jason's. "Have a nice evening, you two. I'll be back late."

"Thanks, Mom." Alex's voice was extra gruff so that *thank you* meant more than just a polite acknowledgment.

"Thanks, Miriam," Jason echoed. "We'll try not to wait up."

She chuckled as she gave Audacity a last scritch, then left them standing awkwardly in the hallway when the door shut behind her. *No. We're not letting this get weird.* Jason slid an arm around Alex's waist and steered him toward the kitchen.

"How about dinner first and you can change and stuff later? You look like you need food."

Alex snuffled at the air, his stomach growling angrily. "Smells so good."

"Great, we all agree—me, you and the savage beast you call a stomach."

That got a soft chuckle, thank God. Jason insisted that Alex have a seat while he brought everything to the table. Alex healed quickly but not *that* quickly and the less he used his poor hands, the better.

Jason set the sliced roast on its bed of carrots, parsnips and celery in the center of the table with the bowl of spinach salad between them. "How're you feeling?"

"They hurt." Alex flexed his hands carefully. "Arm's worse, though. How's yours?"

"Had worse." The burn ached more than anything. He couldn't compare it to Alex's impaled arm. He set Audacity's special plate at her place with its tiny pieces of meat just in time for her to scramble up onto her cushions. "We'll have some interesting scars from this."

"Yeah."

Okay, conversation dead end there. He let Alex eat in peace for a bit since that worked best and Alex was attacking dinner like he hadn't seen food for months. Jason hid a grin in a bite of carrot. He didn't have to ask if it was good. Alex's pleased little growls were more than enough compliment.

Just as Jason worried that he was going to have to start a pull-a-sentence-at-a-time-out-of-Alex campaign, Alex put his fork down.

"The thing we were talking about before the drop bears screwed up a nice lunch."

"Yes." Jason sat straight, funneling all his attention to Alex.

"I've thought. A lot. About what I thought you were saying that first night and what you probably meant instead."

"Okay?"

"Yeah." Alex stared at his empty plate. "I... When you first said it? I thought you were saying I *should* see other people. That *we* should. It confused me and it... Um, it hurt."

"I know, babe. I'm sorry." Jason stopped himself from babbling on since Alex obviously had more to say.

"Pretty sure you weren't trying to push me away when I started thinking about it." The plate staring continued but Alex was still going. "So I understood the *what* but I still didn't get the *why*."

Jason reached across and gripped Alex's forearm since holding hands wasn't an option. "It's been hard for me to understand, too. Jealous. Worried that my family being awful to you was pushing you away. I've never been jealous before. My previous relationships — I just wasn't and I didn't care what my family thought about them."

"Okay. That makes sense. But you've also said they don't last very long. Your relationships." Finally, Alex looked up and his next words were soft, tentative. "I kinda want this to last."

"Me too. Like I've never wanted anything else."

Alex nodded, as if that was a confirmation he'd needed. "I figured you thought I wanted Captain Valbuena since I was letting him feed from me. Sure, he's sexy and he *did* want me. Not something he was shy about."

"See, that's what—"

"But, um… I like him. Just not to have sex with. For lots of reasons. Most important… No, not most important. Reason would be 'cause I didn't want him back. But he's also a superior and a vampire—"

Jason frowned. "You have a problem with vampires?"

"Not as people. But he's so cold. Doesn't appeal to me." Alex eyed the serving plate. "Do you mind if I eat some more?"

"Of course not. I think your daughter wants more, too."

Mrrraaah. Audacity directed her plaintive call at her empty plate.

"Okay. So I figured that was easy. I'd just tell you I wasn't interested in him." Alex slid the tiny pieces he'd cut onto Audacity's plate before he served himself seconds. "But then I started to wonder if there were other reasons you thought I'd want to see the captain. Maybe I'm way off. But I think part of it's because of the difference… The… Saying *superpowers* sounds so dumb. The stuff I do better than humans do. That vampires do better, too. Maybe you thought I wanted someone stronger."

That little insight was far too close to the truth. "I didn't—"

"Hmm. I think you did," Alex murmured around a bit of pot roast.

"All right, yes." Jason shoved his own plate away, no longer hungry. "I worry that someday you'll look at me and just see a potbellied, underachieving dogcatcher."

Alex stopped chewing for a second as if that gave him pause. Then he nodded and went back to eating. "Even worse than I thought. I'm going to say some things and you're not allowed to argue. No saying *but, Alex*. Or telling me I might be wrong. Because this is how I feel."

Jason cringed. *Do I do that?* "Okay?"

"I don't want anyone else. I want you. I'm still a wolf, even if I'm human and it means I'm not good at having more than one partner. Can't help that." Alex speared a carrot and gestured with it in little jabs toward Jason. "Also, I love your body, so stop trying to tell me I shouldn't. I don't want anyone faster or stronger. You keep calling me a hero? Who was it that saved us at Pecca's house? Who crawled through all the weird missiles and the magic with nothing but a chair and a tray to take out those creatures?"

"I... It was..." Jason blinked at him, completely thunderstruck.

"Heroic. You should be getting the commendation, not me. You're kind and warm. You care about all the people, not just the human ones. And you're brave every single day when you have to deal with dying mama cats and the terrible things people do to animals. I'd cry way too much every night if I had your job."

"I do what I love, so it's not that hard. Not every day's horrible and sad."

Alex squeezed his hand, despite the bandages. "I still couldn't do it. Anyway." He popped his carrot pointer into his mouth and chewed for a moment, probably herding his thoughts back together. "I'm saying you're plenty strong and heroic and I don't need anyone who can outrun me or out-wrestle me. I need you."

"I love you so much, you know that, right?" Jason put his head on Alex's arm, needing to be closer.

Alex made an odd sound in his chest, sort of a whimper-growl. "I know. I love you, too."

Jason closed his eyes, drinking in Alex's warmth as he went on, "You're all I need. You're all I want. I don't see that changing."

"Okay," Alex whispered. "You think, um...? Can we clean up later?"

The husk in Alex's voice made Jason lift his head. *Was that a proposition?* The banked fire in Alex's eyes said, oh, heck yes, it was. "Let me just put the roast back in the pot so your daughter doesn't get ideas. Meet you upstairs?"

Alex looked down at his uniform and muttered, "Maybe give me a couple." He didn't exactly run upstairs, but he moved with purpose.

The shower ran, so Jason took his time and cleaned up anyway. He had dinner leftovers put in the fridge and the dishwasher loaded by the time the water turned off upstairs. *Perfect.* Especially since he'd gotten cleaned up and ready to go before Alex had gotten home.

With one towel wrapped around his waist and another toweling his thick mane of silver and black, Alex wandered out of the steam as Jason reached the top of the stairs. The bruises and the handful of small burns concerned him but Alex would just get annoyed if he mentioned them. *His poor hands, though.*

"Let's rewrap those first," Jason suggested.

"They're not that bad."

"Babe, they look like the Tasmanian Devil thought they were chew toys."

Alex sighed but he gave Jason the few precious minutes it took to re-bandage both his hands and his arm. Apparently, Alex's patience ran out the second Jason fastened the last piece of tape. He wrapped his arms around Jason, trapping him against the back of the bathroom door, and seized Jason's mouth in a hungry kiss. Jason yelped in surprise, then leaned into the starved assault, running his hands down Alex's spine to cup his muscular butt.

"Hmm. Bed? Didn't really have getting fucked against a door in mind." *And your hands would just tear open.*

"Bed," Alex growled in his ear as he did a lift and turn to get Jason away from the door.

If it'd been his own house, Jason would've been shedding clothes on the way to the bedroom. Since that wasn't exactly something he wanted Miriam to come home to, he waited until his feet hit the soft carpet of Alex's room before he started stripping. He closed the door behind him—Audacity knew by now to amuse herself for a bit when the door was closed—and basked in the heat of Alex's eyes as he undressed. Good thing he was barefoot. He was far too impatient for socks.

Naked, his erect cock out in front, he stalked to the bedside and hooked a finger under the towel Alex still wore.

"Not the proper uniform of the day, Officer," he whispered against Alex's throat, thrilled with the hitch of breath he received.

"No?"

"Oh, no, not at all." Jason gave a hard yank and flung the towel across the room, Alex's hard breaths sliding into growls as Jason ran his hands down his ribs to grasp his hips. "Much better."

Alex bent to nuzzle and lick at Jason's throat, his need to reconnect with scent and taste so familiar as a prelude to sex by now that it set off showers of lightning strikes in Jason's core. He turned them slowly, backing Jason up until he sat on the bed, then kept coming as Jason lay back to take Alex between his thighs.

Once his hands hit the bed for balance, though, Alex hissed. Not the good kind of hiss, either. The *oh, crap that hurts* kind.

"Okay, hold up." Jason helped him sit back and get the weight off his hands. "No reason we have to do it that way." He wrapped both arms around Alex and flipped him onto his back. "Better?"

"Yeah." Alex managed a little smile with the growl, so it must've been a lot better.

"Good." Jason leaned down to nibble at Alex's earlobe. "Gonna ride you like one of those drugstore ponies."

Alex snickered. "*That* was your best analogy?"

"Hey, I got you to laugh, didn't I?" Jason worked his way down the thick column of Alex's neck, down to his furry chest, sucking and licking until he could tug at one dark nipple with his teeth. Alex moaned and his hips bucked toward the ceiling, his erection bumping against Jason's ass.

"Whoa. Easy there, big fella," Jason gave his side a couple of sturdy pats as if he were a prize stallion.

"I've read about ponies. Not that I'd want that."

"You're so damn cute when you blush."

Jason reached back for Alex's cock, rolling the foreskin as he shifted into position. Alex tried to help and Jason batted his hands away, though he allowed Alex to rest them on his hips. Even through the bandages, the heat Alex gave off was impressive.

While he'd gotten himself ready as the roast simmered, in an excess of optimism that everything would be okay, a little extra lube was never a bad thing when dealing with Alex's size. Jason reached for it on the shelf over the headboard and soon had Alex moaning and thrashing as he spread the cool slick down Alex's cock.

That moment of *holy fuck that's never going to fit* passed as the head slipped inside and Jason sank down, watching Alex's eyes widen as he took him down to his base. Yeah, it was a little much, but it felt so good, too, having Alex impale him.

"You okay?" Alex whispered.

"Split in half by a redwood log." Jason curled over to kiss him and take Alex's bottom lip between his teeth. "But it's amazing. You. You're amazing."

He knew that rumble, knew the hard tightening of Alex's arms around him. His wolf was beyond waiting and Alex took him by the hips and thrust up. Jason held on to the headboard and caught his rhythm. Not the gentle, tender lovemaking they sometimes needed, no. This was hard and fast, Alex's thrusts just short of savage and what they both desperately needed right then.

My Alex, my half-wild, wonderful Alex.

Jason freed a hand from the headboard to stroke his cock hard. He didn't want Alex holding back and waiting. Caught between the heavy pounding on his gland and the tight friction of his fist, his orgasm built hot and swift, a tidal wave of pleasure that crested and crashed as he bellowed out his climax, hot streamers of white decorating the fur on Alex's chest.

Alex let out a hard huff and thrust harder, his rhythm breaking and stuttering as he gasped and cried out his own orgasm a few thrusts later.

They stilled, Jason clinging to the headboard, head hung between his shoulders, Alex breathing so hard he wheezed. No, wait. He was laughing. Wheeze-laughing.

"What?" Jason cracked an eye open to see Alex grinning.

"Just wondering if I was a drugstore pony, where you would put the coins."

"Pfff. I think *that* should be obvious."

Of course, Alex just laughed harder and Jason had to dismount before he was thrown, Alex's cum trickling down his thigh. That was all right. More than all right. He nudged Alex over so he could nestle close, sleepy and overjoyed to be back in his wolf's arms.

"Hmm. That was perfect," Alex murmured against Jason's hair.

"Thanks. You weren't bad yourself." He chuckled as Alex gave him a desultory slap on his ass. "Should I open the door for her majesty?"

"Couple minutes. Too comfortable."

"Alex?"

"Hmm?"

"Does it bother you? That I'll probably always just be an animal control officer? That I don't have any ambition?"

"No. Is it supposed to? You do something you're good at and you're helping. Helping doesn't seem a big thing with a lot of ambitious people, does it? I'll probably always just be a police officer." Alex stilled for a moment, the bit of tension in his muscles signaling a thought occurring. "Though they might start letting us test for detective soon. Maybe. Captain said he'd see what he could do."

"Really? That's great. You should do it."

"Me? No. I mean Kash had already made detective, so he should. And Jeff, too. And Carr, 'cause he almost was."

"But who was it that put everything together this time? Not them. You."

Alex gave a one-shouldered shrug under Jason's head. "Maybe someday. I need to understand better what it means and what I'd have to do for testing. Right now, I'm happy doing what I do."

"As long as you're not selling yourself short."

"No. I know it takes me more time to work up to things. Maybe I'll get there someday." A frown colored Alex's voice. "Right now, there's bigger stuff going on. Stuff that'll take people like Kash to figure out. Why someone keeps coming after us and who they are. I mean, what the hell have we ever done to them?"

"If it's even the same person." Jason had no illusions about this stalker mage or mages giving up. Something else weird and horrible was bound to come along soon. Later for all that.

"Yeah. For now I could use a few weeks of false alarm alien calls." Alex hugged him tighter and kissed the top of his head. "And you."

"Oh, well. That last part I can totally help with." Jason snuggled closer and threw an arm across Alex's barrel chest. "And Alex? You know I'm not going to let my family chase you away, right? I mean, we both know I'm never going to tell my family to fuck off. But I'm not going to get bullied into choosing you or them. I need both."

Alex hugged him hard, his breath hitching suspiciously. "Okay. I'm...okay."

He might've been just ordinary Jason but he had his wolf-hero to come home to most nights, a hero who loved him and his ordinariness. That was more than enough to keep his heart secure and whole.

A sudden battering of tiny paws sounded on the bedroom door.

Miw. Mee-eew. Miiiiw!

Jason chuckled as he rolled out of bed to open the door. *And a kitten princess prodigy to answer to.* So much more than any other mere mortal could expect out of life.

* * * *

The week had been quiet but Wolf couldn't shake a heavy pall of dread that had nothing to do with stalker mages or strange entities. Jason had said they were going to a family dinner at his parents' house that Saturday. While he knew he couldn't avoid these possible confrontations forever, he really would rather have faced a giant snapping turtle-pill bug hybrid ridden by rabid dust bunnies with drop bear minions.

Maybe.

At least he wasn't going on his own this time. He helped Jason carry food containers out to the truck and tried to tell himself that the worst Jason's family could do was be mean to him. In a way, that was fine, but he didn't always understand human meanness and his anxiety already lodged heavy and painful in his chest.

"It'll be all right, hon." Jason gripped his thigh before they drove down the hill. "They need to see that we can't get scared off. That I'm not hiding you."

"Can I hide if I feel like it?"

"If it gets that bad, we'll leave. Deal?"

"Deal."

Jason kept a running monologue, cheerful and comforting, as they drove over since Wolf's words deserted him. The reception at the house was predictably cold, with Jason's mom glaring hostile daggers his way as she let them in. The dynamics inside the house were eerily consistent with the first time he'd met the family, with the father and siblings occupying the front room. Again, Lisa separated herself from the mass of unwelcoming eyes to greet him, though this time Julia and Daniel joined her.

Wolf did manage a few sentences, though coherence didn't quite happen, before he retreated farther into the house. Maybe he should have stayed with Jason, who had planted himself in the middle of the living room, arms crossed over his chest as he glowered at his family, but all of Wolf's supposed courage had deserted him.

He found himself in the kitchen, where he nearly tripped over Jason's grandmother, who bustled about from fridge to counter. She gave him a hard side-eye but otherwise ignored him as if he weren't important enough to insult today. She was far too busy.

At one point, she opened a cabinet and frowned at the top shelf, where a set of glass bowls sat far above her head. She grumbled and hurried over to retrieve a step stool from the wall but Wolf thought he could at least save her the trouble.

He pulled the set of four bowls down — they would've been too heavy for her at any rate — and held them out to her. "Ma'am? Which one did you need?"

Still regarding him sideways, she pulled out the second smallest and waited for Wolf to replace the others and retreat before she returned to her cooking. A few minutes later, she retrieved a package of ground meat from the fridge and frowned back up at the bowls. Again, Wolf took them down and held the stack while she chose the third largest.

She mixed spices and other things into the meat with her hands, which she regarded with annoyance when she apparently needed something else. With a few sharp words, she pointed to another cabinet. Wolf opened it for her, his hand hovering over spice containers until she indicated he had the right one. Then she wanted a pitcher from that top shelf. He dutifully retrieved that, as well.

Bedevilment sparked in her eyes as she began to point and demand things from places she couldn't reach — cabinets, the top of the refrigerator, pots from the rack above the center island. Wolf soon caught on that she didn't need any of these things. She was simply seeing if he would fetch them for her. He complied without showing any sign of impatience. What else did he have to do, after all?

She pointed to a top shelf stacked with heavy ceramic plates and bowls of various sizes. He tried to determine what specific item she wanted, pointing to one after the other, but she kept shaking her head. Finally, he took the whole stack of plates in one hand and the group of bowls in the other, probably something he shouldn't have been able to do if he were fully human and brought the entire contents of the shelf down to hold out to her.

Her eyes crinkled at the corners and a small miracle occurred. She laughed. Helplessly. To the point where she was clinging to his forearm to stay upright while Wolf still held the heavy dishes, waiting. Finally, she stepped away, still chuckling and shaking her head, and waved a hand at the dishes. He took it as a sign to put them back and she didn't object when he did. One by one, she began waving away the items she'd asked for that she hadn't needed.

Just as Wolf had placed the last of the unnecessary objects back in its proper place, Julia came into the kitchen.

"I wondered where you got to." She gave Wolf a wry smile.

Her grandmother spoke several rapid sentences to her and while her words were sharp, she still laughed. Julia didn't quite join her but her smile blossomed, bright and relieved.

"*Nai nai* says you may be a demon, but you're the most helpful demon she's ever met. She says you're welcome in the kitchen whenever you like, since you don't get underfoot like certain other men would."

"That's good?" Wolf swallowed hard, his heart still hammering from the surreal exchange. "I mean, I don't like being a demon..."

"She likes you, Alex." Julia took him by the arm and steered him toward the doorway. "I'm not sure she's liked anyone else's significant other this quickly. She still doesn't really like Paul's wife and it's been ten years."

"Oh."

He let her lead him even though he really didn't want to go back into the den of angry humans yet. When they reached the front room, the obvious scene of confrontation there made him want to tuck tail and run back to the kitchen. Jason stood still, not one bit more relaxed than when Wolf had left the room.

"You do whatever you want, Dad," Jason was saying, his voice brittle but steady. "This isn't a phase. I'm not changing. I'm not suddenly going to start seeing girls to please you. And I'm not giving up Alex."

His father snorted. "If you're choosing him over us—"

"No. Dad, no. I'm not playing that game. I'm not choosing him over you. I'm not choosing you over him. This is how it's going to be." Jason's chin came up, a picture of brave defiance. "You don't want Alex in your house? Fine. That makes me angry, but it's your house. But don't expect me to disappear from your lives or pretend you don't exist. Don't expect me to stop being your son or a big brother or Uncle Jason to the kids. Alex is part of my life. You either accept that and try to be civil at least, or you're just going to have to deal with the fact that I have another part of my life that will sometimes take precedence over you."

Wolf snapped his mouth shut, realizing he'd been gaping. He was peripherally aware that everyone had turned to stare at him with Julia on his arm but his focus was on Jason, courageous and proud in the center of the brewing storm. All that came out was, "Um...I don't..."

"Alex, I think we're leaving. I'm not putting you through this."

Angry Mandarin came from behind Wolf as Jason's grandmother nearly plowed over him to shout at the gathered family, shaking a paring knife with every few syllables. Jason's parents tried to get a few words in but she wasn't having it. By the time his grandmother had finished and returned to the kitchen, most of the family was staring uncomfortably at the floor and Jason was the one who gaped in shock.

"Huh. *Nai nai* has spoken," he said to Wolf. "She says you're staying and that's that. Though she still called you a demon."

"That's okay," Wolf said softly. "I think I understand how she means it now. I don't mind."

Maybe it wouldn't be a comfortable afternoon. Maybe Jason's parents would never fully accept him, but Jason had braved the family's wrath and had stood up for him, for them, and Wolf had never been prouder of anyone.

Human families were complicated, some more than others, but if Jason could have enough courage to stand his ground, the least Wolf could do was stand with him. He made his way over and took Jason's hand to stand beside him where he belonged.

"I know..." Wolf struggled for words and Jason squeezed his hand. "I'm not part of this p—family. I know I might never be and might not be welcome here. But you worry about Jason. I worry about him, too. Jason's the most amazing person I've ever met. He cares about everything. I've never seen anyone care so...completely."

"Alex," Jason whispered and shook his head.

"Stuff will happen to hurt him. Even I know that. Maybe I will sometimes." Wolf drew himself up. "But I'll still be there for him. I won't break his heart."

Paul's jaw remained clamped, his gaze actively hostile, but Mr. and Mrs. Shen had relaxed, studying him, considering.

"Stay, Officer Wolf," Mrs. Shen said, her words soft and even. "Have dinner with us. But I'm watching you."

"Yes, ma'am. Of course."

Wolf's stomach chose that moment for a loud growl and the tableau broke up abruptly as Mrs. Shen hurried off to the kitchen. Lisa and Julia followed, snagging Jason and Wolf along the way. Plating and table setting followed at a whirlwind pace with Wolf finishing one task only to find something else thrust into his hands.

None of the imperious commands annoyed him at all. He was included in the dance. Even if his entrance into this pack was provisional, they were letting him play a part at the heart of things. Even better, Jason smiled and laughed with his sisters, his mother and grandmother, happier than Wolf had seen him in weeks.

He'd always known that for a man like Jason, pack was everything and now his heart warmed almost to melting. He'd helped his Jason come home.

About the Author

The unlikely black sheep of an ivory tower intellectual family, Angel Martinez has managed to make her way through life reasonably unscathed. Despite a wildly misspent youth, she snagged a degree in English Lit, married once and did it right the first time, (same husband for almost twenty-four years) gave birth to one amazing son, (now in college) and realized at some point that she could get paid for writing.

Published since 2006, Angel's cynical heart cloaks a desperate romantic. You'll find drama and humor given equal weight in her writing and don't expect sad endings. Life is sad enough.

She currently lives in Delaware in a drinking town with a college problem and writes Science Fiction and Fantasy centered around gay heroes.

Angel Martinez loves to hear from readers. You can find her contact information, website details and author profile page at http://www.pride-publishing.com.